Maps to Nowhere

Also by Marie Brennan

The Memoirs of Lady Trent
A Natural History of Dragons
The Tropic of Serpents
Voyage of the Basilisk
In the Labyrinth of Drakes
Within the Sanctuary of Wings

Turning Darkness Into Light

Onyx Court
Midnight Never Come
In Ashes Lie
A Star Shall Fall
With Fate Conspire
In London's Shadow: An Onyx Court Omnibus

Driftwood
The Night Parade of 100 Demons

Rook and Rose
(as M.A. Carrick)
The Mask of Mirrors
The Liar's Knot

Wilders
Lies and Prophecy
Chains and Memory

Doppelganger
Dancing the Warrior
Warrior
Witch
A Doppelganger Omnibus

Varekai
Cold-Forged Flame
Lightning in the Blood

Collections
Ars Historica
Down a Street That Wasn't There
Monstrous Beauty
Never After
The Nine Lands

Nonfiction
Dice Tales
Writing Fight Scenes
New Worlds, Year One
New Worlds, Year Two
New Worlds, Year Three

Maps to Nowhere

MARIE BRENNAN

Copyright © 2017 Bryn Neuenschwander

All rights reserved, including the right to reproduce this book, or portion thereof, in any form.

This is a work of fiction. Any references to historical events, real people, or real locales are used fictitiously. Other names, characters, places, and incidents are the product of the author's imagination, and any resemblance to actual events or locales or persons, living or dead is entirely coincidental.

First published 2017 by Book View Café Publishing Cooperative.
304 S. Jones Blvd. Ste# 2906
Las Vegas, Nevada 89107
http://bookviewcafe.com

Print edition 2021
ISBN 978-1-61138-952-4

"Once a Goddess" was first published in *Clockwork Phoenix 2*, ed. Mike Allen, July 2009. "The Mirror-City" was first published in *Clockwork Phoenix 5*, ed. Mike Allen, April 2016. "A Mask of Flesh" was first published in *Clockwork Phoenix*, ed. Mike Allen, July 2008. "But Who Shall Lead the Dance?" was first published in *Talebones* #34, February 2007. "A Thousand Souls" was first published in *Aberrant Dreams*, February 2007. "Beggar's Blessing" was first published in *Shroud Magazine* #2, spring 2008. "Nine Sketches, in Charcoal and Blood" was first published in *On Spec* #70, November 2007. "Letter Found in a Chest Belonging to the Marquis de Montseraille Following the Death of That Worthy Individual" was first published in *Abyss & Apex*, January 2009. "From the Editorial Page of the Falchester Weekly Review*" was first published in Tor.com, April 2016. "Love, Cayce" was first published in *Intergalactic Medicine Show* #22, April 2011.

Contents

Foreword	7
Once a Goddess	9
The Mirror-City	27
A Mask of Flesh	35
But Who Shall Lead the Dance?	49
A Thousand Souls	55
Beggar's Blessing	59
Nine Sketches, in Charcoal and Blood	69
Letter Found in a Chest Belonging to the Marquis de Montseraille Following the Death of That Worthy Individual	87
From the Editorial Page of the *Falchester Weekly Review*	93
Love, Cayce	101
Afterword	119
Story Notes	121

Foreword

There are five basic schools of thought on the topic of author commentary in a short story collection: 1) put it all together at the front; 2) all together at the back; 3) individually before each story; 4) individually after each story; and 5) don't bother.

For the ebook editions of these collections, I can leverage the format to facilitate multiple approaches, by linking to the notes at the end of each story while collecting the notes themselves at the end of the book. Alas, dead trees are not so flexible, which means I have to pick. You will find all the story notes following the Afterword, and can time your reading of them as you choose.

This collection contains ten stories, all of them set in worlds other than our own. They are organized into a few general groupings: the first three are somewhat anthropological in nature, exploring invented cultures; the next three are more folkloric, playing with tropes from fairy tales and legends; the three after that are historically flavored, though not set in real locations or time periods. Overlapping that, the latter two historical-ish tales are epistolary (consisting of letters), as is the final story in the collection. I hope you enjoy them!

Once a Goddess

FOR ELEVEN YEARS Hathirekhmet was a goddess, and then they sent her home.

She didn't understand. They explained it to her, in patient tones just bordering on the patronizing, and she didn't understand. They told her, again and again, right up until the moment it ended, because they had done this before and they knew the goddess never understood.

She didn't believe them until the ceremony, when a little girl with wide, dark eyes came into the sanctum and touched her on the brow. That little girl, blessed with the seventeen signs of perfection, was Hathirekhmet now.

After eleven years, she who had been Hathirekhmet was Nefret again—and then they sent her home.

They said the woman in the wattle-and-daub house was her mother. And Nefret accepted it, numbly, as she had accepted everything since that little girl took her place.

No—not her place. Hathirekhmet's place, and she was Hathirekhmet no more; that honor passed now to another, as it always did. They told her to be proud; eleven years was a long time. Few girls retained their perfection for so long. Most ceased to be the goddess much younger.

The woman in the house no more knew what to do with Nefret than Nefret knew what to do with herself. She introduced herself as Merentari, and the two of them embraced while the priests looked on with benevolent smiles, but it was brief and unbearably awkward. They parted, and did not touch again.

Slaves carried the priests' litters away, and the plainer one Nefret had occupied. And that simply, the last vestige of her temple life was gone.

But casting off that life was not so easily done. "You are dusty from the road; no doubt you wish to bathe," Merentari said, and Nefret stood dumbly, waiting for slaves to come and wash her. "I have prepared food; please, eat," Merentari said, and Nefret stared at the spiced paste and flatcakes laid before her, the small bowl of dried figs. "You will sleep here, with me," Merentari said, and Nefret turned her face from the straw mattress, willing herself not to cry.

Hathirekhmet did not choose her vessels according to caste. The seventeen signs of perfection could appear in the meanest hovel as easily as the imperial palace. As indeed they had, eleven years before.

Awkwardness gave way to rage quickly enough. Nefret was accustomed to luxury, servitude, and instant obedience. She did not know how to do the simplest of chores, and became furious when Merentari tried to teach her. "Wash these dishes," Merentari said, and Nefret slapped them from her hands. "Sweep the floor," Merentari said, and Nefret hurled the broom out the door. "Bring in more dung for the fire," Merentari said, and Nefret fled the house.

Had her father been alive, she would have been curbed quickly enough. No woman so useless would ever be bought as a wife; she had to learn a wife's place and a wife's skills, soon, before age rendered her a spinster. Nefret's father would have beaten the wilfulness out of her, rather than abandon her to that fate. But he died two years after she became the goddess' avatar. She had no memory of him, no more than she did of Merentari.

Huddled in the lee of the riverbank, out of the punishing sun and free, however briefly, of the life that now trapped her, Nefret entertained a vision of something different. The priests said this woman was her mother, but what if they lied? Surely Hathirekhmet would not have abandoned her to this, to flies and dust and fires built of dung. For eleven years Nefret had been her vessel; did that mean nothing to the goddess now?

Tears leaked from beneath Nefret's tightly closed lids, tracking through the grime on her cheeks and falling to the thirsty earth, where they vanished without a trace.

Merentari's younger brother found her there a short while later, and dragged her back to the house. He was not cruel, but he tolerated no resistance, and there were marks on her arm when he finally released her inside the hut. Merentari scowled, her patience worn thin by Nefret's intransigence. "There you are. Get washed up, and quickly; we don't want to miss this chance."

A tub of water waited out back, and a hard-bristled brush that Merentari used to scrub Nefret clean. Her brisk ministration was as unlike the gentle service of the slaves as the dull, repetitive food was to the feasts of the temple, but it did the work; Nefret was as clean as she'd been since coming to this place she refused to call home. Her mahogany skin glowed, and Merentari scraped her thick hair back into two braids so tight they made Nefret's head ache. Instead of Merentari's cast-off clothing, she wore a thin robe she had never seen before, plain, but neatly pleated, and of good linen.

When Nefret was clean and dressed, Merentari took her roughly by the chin and forced the girl to look at her. Taller than this woman they said was her mother, Nefret felt calm superiority envelop her. She might be in exile, but she still had her pride.

"You keep your mouth shut, except when he asks you a question," Merentari said. "You be polite and meek. This might be your one chance at any kind of future, girl. If you spit on this, you'll end your days as a beggar in the streets. Understand?"

Nefret did not, but she learned quickly enough. A man came to inspect her—Nefret's mind would not let go of that word. *Inspect*, as a temple servant might inspect a cow offered for sacrifice. There were men, it seemed, who would pay a good bride-price for a woman who was once a goddess, men interested enough in prestige that they did not care how bad a wife they bought.

Nefret kept her mouth shut, but not for the reasons her mother might have wished. She feared she would be sick. Reduced to this, after the life she had lived: bought and sold, like livestock. The man did not speak to her at all, questions or otherwise. When his inspection was done, he turned to Merentari. "Can she cook? Weave? Sew?"

Lying was not among Merentari's talents. Her hesitation was answer enough.

"I didn't expect it," the man said. His own robe was finely woven, edged with azure embroidery. Such as he would have some servants, possibly even slaves. Wealth, by the standards of this hovel. "Teach her basic domestic duties. If she passes muster by flood-time, I'll buy her."

Merentari's weathered face showed gratitude that bordered on fawning. She was not old, but hard work had aged her young. Beauty was a luxury few peasants could afford. "Yes, noble one. Thank you. I will make sure she learns."

When the wealthy man was gone, Merentari turned to her daughter. "You *will* learn. Or you will starve."

In the dark hours before dawn, when Nefret so frequently lay awake, she knew that Merentari did not mean to make her suffer. The woman was harsh because there was no other choice; she did not want her daughter to end like this, scraping the barest existence out of the hard-packed dirt. Pity would not buy her a better future.

In the bright hours of day, Nefret hated her mother with a passion she fancied rivaled the rages of Hathirekhmet herself.

Merentari bent grimly to the task of making her daughter into a suitable wife. A thick reed from the riverbank became an all too familiar fixture in Merentari's hand, laying burning lines across Nefret's back when she rebelled. Never before had she been beaten; rarely had she even suffered pain, and then slaves had raced to bring soothing ointment, tea to numb her senses. Pride kept Nefret's jaw clenched; she cried out the first few times, but soon forbade herself such weakness.

She tried—if only because it was a path for her to follow, and promised a life more like the one she knew. But the shuttle and thread were alien in her hands, the cook-fire smoky and foul. Other girls learned these skills from childhood, practicing them for years under their mothers' eyes. The priests had taught Nefret all the wrong things, and then dropped her into a life for which she was wholly unprepared.

She tried, and she failed, until one day she could endure no more and ran away again, her feet this time taking her in a new direction.

Nefret smelled the market before she saw it, a confusing welter of dust and sweat, food and animal dung. She crested a rise and saw the clustered buildings, mud brick structures huddled up against each other, with sun-bleached awnings branching out from their walls. A market was a recognizable thing to her, though this one was shabby and small. She had gone through markets before, during festival processions.

Her bare feet led her down the slope and toward the market as if of their own accord.

At first no one noticed her. Nefret felt like a ghost, drifting down the strip of sunlight between the awnings on either side. Silent amidst the market's clamor, she could almost believe she didn't exist. But this was a small market; strangers were rare, and even moreso strangers like her, beautiful and unweathered by a peasant's hard life. A middle-aged woman bent to whisper to another, and then someone else pointed, and little by little, the market fell into stillness.

The stillness was broken by a young woman who hesitated at the edge of the crowd, then darted forward and flung herself facedown onto the hard-packed soil at Nefret's feet. "Mistress of the desert winds," she said, her voice ragged and unclear, "bless me, I beg you."

The words struck Nefret like the chilled water the slaves poured over her for the Ceremony of the River's Coming. Her fingers twitched, reflexively: in learning to weave, they had not forgotten how to form the sign of blessing.

But she was not the goddess.

She ached to reach out, to make the sign above the young woman's head, perhaps even to move her foot forward so the supplicant could kiss it. To these people, she was not Nefret, daughter of nobody; she was Hathirekhmet, the Divine Face, the Sand-Mother. Relentless and harsh as the desert and sun, but not without mercy.

But she was not Hathirekhmet. Not anymore. To bless this young woman would be blasphemy.

The magnitude of her loss gaped before her, stretching into the endless distance like the desert itself, even more barren of life.

Nefret stared down at the young woman, stricken and shaking, while the silence stretched tighter and tighter. Then she spun without a word and fled, back to the house, to weep for her loss where no one could see.

But Merentari was waiting for her there, reed switch in hand and fury on her face.

Nefret stopped dead, facing the woman in the doorway. Her mother, they said, and to deny it was childish. A peasant, whose daughter was born with the seventeen signs the priests looked for. An ordinary woman, whose ambition could rise no higher than to sell that same daughter to a man that wanted for his wife a woman who was once a goddess.

That man—she did not even know his name—wanted her for who she had been. No: for who she was now, the loss she had suffered. Hathirekhmet he feared, but Nefret he could own.

To go into his house would mean accepting that her loss was her only value now.

"I am not Hathirekhmet," Nefret said to her mother. The words came out steady, with a deadness that could pass for calm. "But I will not sell myself as her leavings."

Merentari's face twisted, as she saw Nefret's one chance—*her* one chance—withering into death. "No one else will take you!"

Nefret nodded, slowly. The logic was inescapable.

"Then no one else will have me," she said. "I would rather be nothing than be his."

Merentari's expression showed that she did not understand. Nefret did not know when her mother realized the truth; by the time it happened, she had turned her back, and walked away from the hut, into the desert.

The sand burned against Nefret's forehead and arms, scorching her body even through the cotton of her robe, cooking the flesh beneath, but she remained motionless, accepting the pain.

In the temple, there were slaves whose sole duty was to stoke the fires beneath raised platforms of sand, so the penitents above continually felt the sun's heat against their bodies. Here, without slaves, the sand grew cool. Nefret rose and crawled sideways, then stretched out again, burning herself anew.

She did not pray. No words could express the screaming need in her heart. She did not know whether she wanted to be purified, made perfect again so she could once more be Hathirekhmet's vessel; to deny and disfigure the flesh that had known divinity and lost it; to die, and feel this pain no more.

All of them. None of them. She did not know.

I would rather be nothing than be his.

She would rather be nothing than what she was now.

When sunset came, the sand chilled quickly. At first it was a pleasant change from the heat of the day; then it became unpleasant, and the desire for self-punishment withered. She rose and walked unsteadily to a rocky upthrust nearby, and there she found a tiny spring; she drained it in moments, then had to wait for the pool to refill. But it was enough to keep her alive.

She did not want to die.

It was more than she had known that morning.

"Very well," Nefret said to the night sky, the pale and envious crescent of Hathirekhmet's younger brother. "I will live. And I will stay alive, until—"

She paused, thinking. Looking at the tiny, glittering pinpricks of the stars, cast off when the moon's folly caused his power to explode outward and be lost.

"Until I am the goddess once more."

They came to her refuge, there among the rocks.

She had not fled so far as to vanish. Men went out into the desert's edge, to hunt lions, to trade with distant oases. They saw her silhouette atop a ridge, or glimpsed her hiding when they came to her tiny spring. A ragged figure, her robe sand-brown with dust, her fine black hair tangled into whips. She was far from perfect now. But Nefret could not regain the qualities she had lost—not now, when blood ran from between her legs, answering the moon's call. If she was to be Hathirekhmet again, she would have to find another way.

So she remembered what the scriptures said about Khapep, how the holy man had survived upon the flesh of lizards and the venom of scorpions, and she learned to do the same. It was bitter fare, even as the desert was bitter, and she welcomed it.

Hathirekhmet was the sun and the sand. Nefret would be the same.

They came to her among the rocks and brought gifts of food, the finest they had to give: dried figs and dates, fish from the river's bounty. But Amuthamse was, the priests said, why Hathirekhmet always withdrew; the goddess departed when the blood came, for it was the sign of the river god's touch. His fertility was alien to Hathirekhmet. Nefret ate scorpions, and left the fish to rot in the sun.

They came for her blessing, and she turned them away. Holy woman? She was no such thing. She would be, someday, and when that dawn came she would extend her hand once more. But until then, she was only Nefret, who let her skin dry out and her hair turn brittle, and tried to remember what she had once known by instinct, by divine grace.

She barely spoke a word until Sekhaf came.

Nefret woke before dawn and went to the spring; she would

drink no more until the sun left the sky. She scooped water into her mouth with dirty hands, wishing she could do without, wondering if that was what Hathirekhmet wanted. Wondering if the goddess would touch her in the instant before death. She was not ready to try, and perhaps that was why she failed.

When she lifted her head, a man sat on a boulder across from her. Nefret heard him approach, but hoped if she ignored him he would go away. He was not a villager, as she had assumed; he wore a traveler's robe and bore a staff, but he did not have the look of a pilgrim. His weathered face was seamed with patient lines.

"Dawn is near," he said—a fact she knew as well or better than he, but he did not have the tone of one lecturing. Rather he seemed to acknowledge the intrusion of his presence. "When it has passed, I hope you will spare me your time."

Nefret's voice came out smoothly from her newly wetted throat, not its usual dry rasp. "I have no blessing to give."

"I do not seek your blessing."

She scowled. "I will not marry you, either."

"I do not seek your hand."

"What, then?"

The lines of his face settled in the pre-dawn light. "Your knowledge."

She stared for a moment, curious against her will. But the sun drew near; she had no time to spare for him. Nefret turned away and climbed the rocks, greeting Hathirekhmet from the pinnacle, basking in this, the goddess' gentlest touch. Soon enough heat would scorch the water from her, as she hunted lizards to eat.

When she descended, the man was still there, patient as stone. "I know nothing," Nefret said, and picked up several likely rocks.

"You know something shared only by a four-year-old girl in a temple," the man said. "You know Hathirekhmet."

Nefret's fingers curled around a sharp-edged fragment of flint. "I *knew* her," she answered, voice roughening to harshness. "She is gone from me now."

The man nodded. "And that makes you unique. Nineteen

years ago, I tried to find her who had been Hathirekhmet, only to discover she had been sold into marriage, to a husband who let her speak to no other. She is dead now, in childbirth. Eleven years ago, I tried again, only to discover she who had been Hathirekhmet hanged herself from her father's great loom. She, too, is dead. There is only you, who understands the goddess better than any man or woman living—who *understands*, but is herself. I cannot ask these questions of Hathirekhmet. I ask them of you." He paused, still seated on his rock. "If you will let me."

The stone hung heavy in her hand. The man's eyes rested unwavering on her—on *her*, Nefret. Who was once a goddess, and for that he valued her. But not like the man Merentari would have sold her to. Her worth lay in what she kept, not what she had lost.

"Ask," she said.

The man stood and bowed his gratitude. "Then I will begin. Of temple life, I have heard; I know the ceremonies and indulgences, the luxury in which the goddess' avatar lives. But only you can tell me: what is the divine presence like?"

The stone fell from Nefret's limp fingers, thudding into the dust. Staring unseeing into the brightening sky, she whispered, "I cannot remember."

It was the truth no one spoke, and Sekhaf believed her. In the early years, Hathirekhmet dwelt often in the body of her avatar, but as the child grew the goddess came less and less. She still performed the ceremonies, for they had merit even if the divine presence had temporarily withdrawn; the avatar was the conduit from earth to heaven. But as Hathirekhmet retreated, the priests began their search for the new vessel. Nefret had not felt the goddess' touch for a year before she left.

Sekhaf sat by as Nefret sliced open the belly of a lizard and said, "Why? Why does she leave?"

He was a philosopher, and did not ask out of cruelty. He had been with her among the rocks for days now, carefully probing, shifting between topics arcane and obvious, questioning everything. Nefret licked the blood from her fingers and answered him. "Amuthamse. A woman is of the river's world, not the desert, and Amuthamse is friend to Hathirekhmet's brother the moon. Once we begin to bleed, we are no longer fit for her presence."

"But you said she leaves earlier, sometimes."

Six months after the last visitation, Nefret had bled for the first time. She had no such name to give herself on that day; the avatar thought of herself as Hathirekhmet, even when the divine presence was not in her. She knew no other identity. But Hathirekhmet did not bleed; Nefret did. She had stayed longer than most, the priests said, her voice remaining high and clear, her skin unblemished, her limbs slender—a far cry from her appearance now. Most girls lost Hathirekhmet sooner, before they ever bled.

"She can sense Amuthamse's approach," Nefret said; it was the answer the priests gave. She could feel Sekhaf's dissatisfaction with it. He loved purity of thought, the clean lines of truth. Anything blurry or untidy displeased him.

No one at the temple thought as he did. They had their scriptures and their answers; they had rituals to carry out, ceremonies to conduct, comforting patterns to shape their lives. None of them had Sekhaf's restless, questioning mind. Nefret did not blame them; she had not questioned, either. Not until the philosopher came.

And his presence, which she had feared would distract her, honed the blade of her own thoughts. If Nefret tested her body less often against the sun, she tested her mind more, contemplating the nature of Hathirekhmet. When Sekhaf went to the village for food, she meditated in silence; when he returned, she had new answers for him, new fragments of memory dredged up from the forgotten corners of the past.

In the desert, there was no time. The rains fell in the mountains and brought the river's flood, Amuthamse's bounty for mankind; Nefret knew nothing of it. The villagers left their offerings and she ignored them, fish bones drying to glass in the sun.

Other men came.

One by one, following word of Sekhaf. Philosophers, men of the mind instead of the temple, their fingers stained from scribing. Some, meaning well, tried to hunt lizards for Nefret, so she might spend more time in thought. Sekhaf taught them better. They waited with patience as she dug out scorpions; they trailed after her in silence as she walked the rounds of her rocks, bare feet hard and cracked as horn against the stone. They did not lust after her, as that man had in Merentari's house; one might as soon lust after the desert. But they asked her questions, and listened when she answered.

"They say it is because we cannot draw near Hathirekhmet ourselves," Nefret said, breaking a new flint to use for butchering lizards. Her hands had turned into bony, calloused things, strong as old leather. The sun warmed her filthy hair. "The ancient priests built a pyramid that reached up to the very sky, seeking the goddess, and were burnt when they climbed to the top. Ordinary people cannot bear her presence and live."

Men both older and younger deferred to Sekhaf here; they spoke among themselves, but only he spoke to Nefret. He said, "But the perfection of her avatars protects them?"

"Imperfections are flaws that can break the vessel," Nefret said, cracking a clean face off the flint. Pottery would be more fitting, but she had no pots out here. "I do not think that is why she takes avatars, though."

The philosopher thought about it. One of the younger men murmured to him, and Sekhaf nodded. "They allow us to experience the divine presence safely. Yet why should that matter to Hathirekhmet? She is the sun's hammer, the desert wind. Humans are not *meant* to be close to such."

Nefret tested the edge of her flint with her thumb, feeling it press against her tough skin. "It is not for us. It is for her, for the goddess—so she may experience the world without destroying it. That is what I think."

Why else should the avatar live so lavishly? She ate foods sweet and spicy, had garments of smooth linen and supple leather and delicate fur. It was a feast of the senses, for one who otherwise could never know such. If the sun descended to earth, she would burn it to a cinder. Hathirekhmet chose avatars because she was curious about the world she saw so far beneath.

Nefret sometimes wondered if the goddess did not envy Amuthamse, who enjoyed all the earth's bounty without fear.

The men whispered to each other, voices rising in excitement. Sekhaf clapped his hands, sharply, and they ceased. "We distract her with our chatter," he said. "Nefret, our thanks. You have given us much to think about. We will return tomorrow."

She rose from her crouch, feeling the flex and contraction of her wiry muscles. A body, imperfect as avatars never were. Yet if the goddess sought sensation, why choose only the slender, the unblemished, the young? There was a whole world of experience, and Hathirekhmet felt only the merest sliver of it. "No," Nefret said. "I will spend tomorrow in contemplation. When I am ready, I will leave a sign for you."

A lizard skull, placed at the foot of the path leading up to her shelter. Nefret had demanded solitude before. Sekhaf bowed. "As you wish."

The others began climbing down the rocks, talking more loudly as they went. Sekhaf stayed, hesitating, until they were well away, and he and Nefret stood alone atop the flint-littered plateau. "You have my thanks as well," he said. Startled, she found herself wondering how long ago the others had come—how long it had been since they were just two, the philosopher and the young woman who was once a goddess. "I came to you hoping to understand something I could never experience for myself. I know now the impossibility of that—but you have given me something far greater. You may not be holy, as Khapep was. But you, Nefret, have wisdom no priest or scripture could ever grant. The world beyond this place will benefit from that wisdom for ages to come."

She blinked eyes dried by sun and wind. That men had come to debate these questions, she knew; she had never thought beyond that. What did the priests think of this woman in the desert, who spoke so familiarly of Hathirekhmet? Did they revere her, as the villagers did? Fear her? Dismiss her as a simple madwoman?

Nefret might have thought herself mad, were it not for Sekhaf. He saw wisdom in her words. But if it was there, they had created it together, questions and answers dancing around and ever closer to the truth.

He bowed and left her, climbing down the rocks after his companions, and not until he was gone did she whisper "thank you" in reply.

She greeted the dawn from the pinnacle of her rocks, as she had for countless days.

The soft breeze of morning blew over her skin, bringing warmth to banish the night's bitter chill. Soon it would be heat, punishing and fierce, growing through the day, until at last the sun retreated, and night claimed the desert once more.

Nefret understood that cycle as well as she did her own body. She knew Hathirekhmet's shifting arc through the sky, and the way the wind answered it; she knew the textures of limestone and flint and the restless dance of the sand.

She knew the seventeen perfections had nothing to do with any of it.

Oh, the priests did not deceive. Those were the sign of Hathirekmet's choice—but the priests mistook the sign for the cause. That certainty had grown in Nefret's heart through all the long debates with the philosophers. The goddess did not occupy a body because it had skin of a particular shade, or a voice of a particular timbre.

If that was not what drew her to a body, then it followed that the loss of those perfections was not why she left.

Something else drove the goddess from her avatars.

This was the question upon which Nefret fixed her mind. She put aside all other thoughts—lizards and scorpions, Sekhaf and the philosophers, Merentari and the man who would have bought her. Nothing but Hathirekhmet. She sat under the eye of the sun, not moving, letting the wind scour her dry. She had drunk no water since the previous dawn, and would drink none until the sun set tonight. She did not seek death—not as she once thought she did—but she seared all the river's gift from herself, the better to know Hathirekhmet.

To know the answer to this one question: why the goddess had left.

The sun beat more strongly upon her with every passing moment. She felt the sweat dry upon her skin, until no more came; she heard the pounding of her own heart, marking the incremental movement of the sun.

And she remembered.

The presence she had gradually lost. The blazing glory of Hathirekhmet, pitiless as stone, but not cruel; cruelty implied a desire for suffering in others. Hathirekhmet did not desire. She simply *was*. And to pour a fragment of herself into an avatar was to be as she otherwise could not be, to feel and see a world otherwise distant to her.

The luxury was the doing of the priests, because they thought the goddess wished it. They honored the one they believed Hathirekhmet's gift to them, thinking it the respectful thing to do.

They did not understand. And Nefret had not, either.

She remembered that blazing presence, annihilating all other thought. As a child it had been easy: she lived in the moment, thinking neither of past nor future. She *was* Hathirekhmet. But as she grew, she changed; thoughts entered her head and did not leave. Dislike of one temple maiden, amusement at an elderly priest. Curiosity about a story from the scriptures. Ideas and feelings, which had to be pushed aside to make room for Hathirekhmet. It grew harder and harder, and the goddess came more rarely.

Because she could not be both Hathirekhmet and herself.

Understanding swirled through the reeling dizziness of her head. The goddess chose children because they were unformed, empty—vessels she could fill. Life was the imperfection, the cracks through which the world entered, changing little girls into young women. And day by day, year by year, the avatars pushed the goddess out to make room for themselves.

Which meant she could undo it. The sun's hammer beat upon her, seeking entrance. All she had to do was step aside, and let the goddess in.

Let go of Nefret, and become Hathirekhmet once more.

Then the goddess could experience something new: a grown body, twisted hard by the desert; a life austere instead of luxurious. Her skin pulsed, a fragile barrier between humanity and divinity. It was easy. Simple. The kind of pure answer Sekhaf sought.

Sekhaf.

She held in the palm of her hand all the things that barred Hathirekhmet from her. All the other thoughts, all the desires and annoyances and knowledge, all the things he called her wisdom. All the things that brought the philosophers to her desert refuge, that fueled their debates in the long heat of day.

Everything that made her who she was.

She could regain what she had lost—by losing what she had gained.

Once, she would have found it no choice at all. Nefret was nothing; Hathirekhmet, everything. But in her seeking, she had found another life. One of lizards and scorpions, a muddy spring and a hard bed, and questions always to be answered. It was not the life she had known in the temple, but it was hers.

Hers. Not Hathirekhmet's.

I was once a goddess. Now I am myself. And myself I shall remain.

Nefret curled her hands around herself, filled her mind with thoughts of life—and bid Hathirekhmet farewell.

She awoke to stone, rough under her cheek and hand.

Nefret opened eyes as dry as dust. She knew without thinking that it was sunset, heat slipping quickly from the air, familiar shadows consuming the world around her.

One shadow was out of place.

She spoke, and the word went little further than her lips. "Sekhaf."

He heard her anyway, or perhaps just saw her move. The

philosopher rose from hiding and came to her side, shame-faced. "I should not have disturbed you," he said. "But I watched from below, and saw you collapse. And I thought—"

For once he did not share his thought. He did not have to. Nefret reached out, and he gave her the skin bag at his side. She drank greedily, tasting the leather, letting water spill over her cheeks and chin.

When at last she stopped, he asked quietly, "Did you find your answer?"

The one she had sought, and more besides. Hathirekhmet bore Nefret no grudge for her choice; a grudge implied desire, and Hathirekhmet desired nothing. Not as a human might.

Not as Nefret desired the life she had chosen to keep.

"I found myself," she said. "That is answer enough."

She could feel Sekhaf's dissatisfaction with it. But that was all right. It was one of his favorite sayings, that questions bred answers, and answers, more questions; he would ask her more before long.

Together they would create wisdom, a new understanding of the goddess. And the time had come, Nefret thought, for that wisdom to go beyond this desert refuge, into the world without. To the priests, and the temple, and the little girl who was Hathirekhmet, who someday would become someone else.

When she did, Nefret would be there to greet her.

The Mirror-City

THE SUN'S RIGHT EYE gazed down upon La Specchia, and its left eye gazed back a thousand-fold, unblinking. Clouds and high winds had blinded those thousand reflected eyes for weeks, ever since the death of the city's ruler; but now the canals and lagoons lay flat and quiet, not a ripple disturbing their mirrored surfaces. The skies were always clear and the winds still when a Giovane met his bride.

Cloth shrouded every reflective surface but the water. In the palazzos of the rich, sumptuous silk brocade had been hung over the expensive glass windows, inside and out. Mirrors stood draped as if awaiting the tailor's measuring tape. Vessels of gold and silver were bundled and tucked away into cabinets, where no trailing edge could slip free and reveal a gleaming curve. Ladies and lords alike put away their jewels, adorning themselves instead with colorful embroidery, silk threads knotted into intricate lace. Even the floors were strewn with fine dust, lest their polished surfaces show too much.

In the houses of their lessers, lesser fabrics sufficed, and the precautions needed were fewer. In the houses of the poor, no draping was needed at all, for they had nothing so fine as to give a reflection.

Except for eyes. Every citizen of La Specchia, from the heights of the palazzos to the depths of the gutters, went about with gaze downcast. For the eyes, they said, were the mirrors of the soul.

One might almost have thought La Specchia a deserted city,

haunted only by banners and bunting, the curtains draping the windows of glass. Here and there, though, the occasional figure moved. A servant, sent on business his lady insisted could not wait. Merchants whose decorations were not yet hung, hurrying to complete their preparations before the city's heart resumed its beat. Death had stopped the blood of life and trade, but soon it would flow once more.

Guards, dressed for today in leather armor and armed with staves, patrolled to ensure no one went too near the water.

The patrols were hardly needed. There were a hundred stories of what would happen if someone chanced to see their reflection too soon on this day, and few of them ended well. The pragmatic tales said the guards would promtly beat the offender to death— if he was lucky. If he was not, then he would die much more slowly, in the dungeons of La Specchia. The sinister tales said the unfortunate soul would lose his mind, or drown, or fall dead of no visible cause. Most foretold doom for the city, and credited past calamities—earthquakes; plagues; destructive storms—to the errant eyes of some careless resident.

Only one story ended well. It was to avoid this fate that Mafeo slipped down an empty street, all but pressing his chest to the wall.

Early in his journey, he had not held back. The front of his doublet bore scuffs and the dangling threads of an absent button, torn off when it caught in the crack of a post. But scraping down the front of a shop like that had made noise, and caught the attention of the shopkeeper inside. The man came out to harangue him, and Mafeo ran—*ran*, as if this were an ordinary day and he could step where he liked without fear. He almost collided with a parapet overlooking a canal before he realized the danger. After that he kept his distance from water and wall alike, to the spaces where an overhanging eave would have sheltered him from rain, on a day when the sky above did not blaze a pure, unsullied blue.

But there were precious few places one could go in La Specchia without risking the water. It surrounded him on all sides, cut across his path without warning. He knew the great canals of the city, but not the backwaters, and time and again what he thought was a sheltered alley dropped down to meet a muddy ditch, or arched over in a narrow footbridge he dared not cross.

And so Mafeo became lost.

He blamed that shopkeeper, and himself for rousing the man's anger to begin with. Had he not fled, he would have found and crossed the Ponte Cieco long since. There was no safety on the other side, but at least he would be farther from danger. Now he did not even know in which direction the Ponte Cieco lay. The sun offered no guidance, for it stood almost at its highest station: the hour drew near.

He should have taken flight days ago. Mafeo was a young man, seventeen years of age; he should have known—*had* known—that he might be chosen. But the possibility was a distant one, so small as to be laughable.

Until the city's ruler died and the moon waned dark, and the youth of the city, every man and maid in their seventeenth year, crafted lantern boats from paper and set them adrift on the lagoon. Mafeo had done it a dozen times before, to celebrate the new year. As they grew older he and his friends placed bets, competing to see whose boat would float the farthest before it sank. It never occurred to him, in his ambition and naïvete, that on this occasion he should craft his vessel with less care than usual.

Maybe it wouldn't have mattered. The priests and priestesses said it was an omen, fate, the mirror's will. Perhaps even his worst effort would have stayed whole, carried out to sea by its own reflection.

No vessel would carry him to safety now. But perhaps if he hid, that would be enough. Once night had fallen…

No. Mafeo heard voices, the tramp of feet. The entire thing had been madness from the start, doomed to failure. The guards had only to ask at the three bridges: the Ponte di Mani, the Ponte di Ambra, and the Ponte Cieco. Few enough people were about, and most of those known to one another; even with gazes downcast, someone would have noticed Mafeo passing by. If he had not crossed any of the great bridges, then he must still be in the heart of La Specchia. From there, they had only to search.

The sounds echoed off the walls and the ever-present water. He could not tell where the guards were, which way to go to avoid them. Mafeo chose his turns at random, pace quickening until he was almost running. Water seemed to be everywhere. Here a gutter; there a silenced fountain, its basin still full. Someone shouted, and he spooked like a cat in the opposite direction.

And there, ahead of him, was the Ponte Cieco.

It rose in geometric perfection, the straight ramp of its central stairs flanked on either side by shops that blocked the view of the canal. These were arrayed in splendor, for soon enough the streets would be filled with all the people of La Specchia, from the eldest to the babes in arms, each one hoping to see good fortune in the water. But that time had not yet come, and for now the bridge held a scant handful of merchants, startled into looking up as Mafeo ran toward them.

If he could clear the bridge's crest before the guards came within sight...

The comandante was no fool. He'd sent his men to patrol the streets, yes—but he had left others behind to block Mafeo's escape.

Even four were enough to cordon off the bottom of the stairs, forming a line close enough that they were sure to catch him if he tried to rush through. From behind Mafeo, more shouts: he needed no glance over his shoulder to tell him that other men were rushing into position, denying his retreat.

They would not kill him. And Mafeo did not want to die. He only wanted to save La Specchia from disaster—the disaster *he* would surely bring, weak and unready as he was. Which meant that only one path remained to him.

Mafeo darted left. It was a risk: the outer stairs of the Ponte Cieco were narrower, scarcely wide enough to let three men pass between shops and parapet. If they tried to stop him—and they would—then either he or the guard would run a great risk of looking upon the water. His only hope was that the guard's fear of the consequences would overcome his determination to do his duty, and in that lapse, Mafeo might slip through.

That guard's devotion never came to the test. As Mafeo ran through the portico at the bridge's crest, he collided with a shopkeeper coming to see what the noise was about.

Mafeo and shopkeeper both went sprawling. Only a quick thrust of Mafeo's hands kept him from cracking his head against the stone balusters of the parapet—and then he looked down, through the gap, and he saw the canal below.

Another face gazed back at him.

The reflection should have been dim and muddied. The waters of La Specchia, no matter how still, were not clean; they should not be able to produce so clear an image, its colors so bright. But today was the day the Giovane met his bride, and Mafeo, in his attempt to flee that duty, had brought himself to it just the same.

It was a face he had glimpsed a hundred times before, but rarely looked upon directly. Why should he look? Only after his lantern boat floated blazing out to sea had Mafeo been named the Giovane; only then did his reflection matter, the Giovane of La Specchia's mirror-city. Her hair was darker, her chin more fierce. She dressed in clothes not much different from the servant's robe he had stolen stole before he fled the palazzo, as if she were born to a lower station than he.

Mafeo had, without realizing it, climbed to his feet and leaned over the parapet. Below him she did the same, echoing his actions in perfect synchrony.

Had she, too, been fleeing through the streets of her home?

They said the citizens of the mirror-city had their own lives; only in the waters of La Specchia's many canals did they reflect their counterparts above. The family she hailed from was not his, and her thoughts today were not his, either. She was as alien to him as the sun: sometimes visible, sometimes not, but never within reach. Mafeo wondered what had brought her there—what events had drawn her away from the Ponte di Mani, where five hundred years of tradition dictated they should meet.

Whatever the answer, it changed nothing. The sun stood high overhead, and here, with only a dozen guards and a handful of shopkeepers to watch, the Giovane would be wed.

Mafeo climbed atop the parapet. No one stepped forward to help him; no one would risk seeing their own mirror-city echo in the waters below. Not until the ceremony was done. As a boy, Mafeo used to believe that whoever first looked in the water on this day would take the Giovane's place. It seemed a grand thing back then. Then he became the Giovane, and it did not seem grand at all—to know that the well-being of La Specchia would rest upon his shoulders, a burden he could not possibly bear.

Until now. Until he stood balanced on the parapet's thin edge, meeting the gaze of the young lady below him, the two drawn together like magnets seeking their mates. He did not know how he would find the strength to do what he must, what his predecessors had done, day and night, without respite, from now until he died.

He knew only that he longed to be complete.

Mafeo spread his arms—she did the same—and as one they fell.

The Perfette rose from the water to the sound of bells. All over La Specchia they rang, above and below…and e knew it was illusion, that one was above and one below, one the truth and the other mere reflection.

But all of La Specchia rejoiced, for it had a ruler, and the two halves were whole once more.

There should have been robes, waiting to receive em on the bank of the canal. There should have been a triumphant parade, an honor guard a thousand strong, priests and priestesses to bless the perfection formed by the unification of the two Giovani. Instead there was a wall covered in the slick growth of weeds, a challenge to the Perfette's grip. E shed the waterlogged clothing that weighed em down, and climbed the wall naked. On the pathway above people were beginning to emerge from their houses, eager to greet their counterparts in the mirror-city. But on this pathway they stopped, gaping, and knelt when they saw their neighbors doing the same—for the Perfette stood before them, dripping with the waters purified by eir marriage, male and female melded into a single harmonious whole.

As La Specchia was whole. Once again trade would flow, the two faces of the city brought together as before. The crowded warehouses would throw open their doors, every lack answered by abundance from the other side. The two realms would prosper, their ruler the gate through which everything passed, the point upon which the city's peace and prosperity balanced. It was a burden too great for one alone to bear…and so Giovane wed Giovane, and in completion found strength.

Soon enough the Perfette was gone, whisked away by guards to eir palazzo, with only a damp patch on the stone to mark where e had stood. But the memory lingered. When the citizens rose from their knees and flocked to the canals to greet their reflections, to celebrate the beginning of a new reign and the renewal of La Specchia's unity, each of them studied well the face in the waters below: women gazing down at men, poor reflected by rich. If they leapt into the canal now, they would only get wet; the moment of transformation had passed. But when they returned to their homes and uncovered their windows, brought out once more their copper pots and silver spoons, they studied their faces in the polished surfaces and remembered perfection.

A Mask of Flesh

SITTING ALONE in the green heat of the forest, far from the road and any observing eyes, Neniza began to craft her mask of flesh.

She started with her toes, for the face would be the hardest part. Toes, feet, legs; the gentle curve of hips. She would have dearly loved to shape for herself the slender, delicate body of an amantecatl, but it would never work. Oh, she could take the form easily enough, but the amanteca were not common caste, and she could never hope to mimic the ways of court folk well enough to pass. Instead she crafted the petite, pretty figure of a young alux peasant. Someone innocent of city ways. Someone who could catch the eye of the lord.

Her father had taught her this work, their art, after her horrified mother saw what she had birthed and left it in the woods. He wished she were still a son, Neniza knew, wished she had not changed into a daughter. Daughters were dangerous things. But his own words had done it, telling the story of what happened to their people. Waking the anger in her. The priests spoke of the wet season and the dry season, the season of giving and the season of taking. For her people, it was no mere abstraction. Their bodies reflected their souls.

Perhaps her father could overlook the wrong they had suffered; Neniza could not. She had not told him where she was going, what she intended to do. He believed they should stay out of sight, accept the hidden existence left to them—never mind that he himself went to town all too often, to court the women of other castes, perhaps to sire more children for them to fear. It was all right for *him*.

But not for her. Not so long as she remained female. She was too dangerous.

That means I'm powerful, Neniza thought, and began to work on her face.

She made it a young one, and attractive, wondering as she did so if it looked anything like her mother. Her father would never say. Neniza had nothing to know her by, no way to pick her mother out of the countless aluxob working the fields, and if she were to go to town without her mask of flesh, her mother would never acknowledge a thing like her as offspring. Every time she made an alux face, she told herself it was her mother's, and every time it was different.

Bushy, soft hair above a round and cheerful face, with eyes the fresh green of new corn. The mask was complete, but Neniza hesitated. Her father would warn her against this, if he knew.

Her father had proved his weakness many times over.

Neniza pulled clothes on over the fleshy nakedness of her body, loincloth, skirt, and a shawl broad enough to hide her arms, then forced her way through the trees to the road.

The city almost made her turn back.

Neniza had been to town before, disguising herself as a woman of one common caste or another, mingling into the crowds she found there, but her first sight of the city showed her how little that had prepared her.

The huge stone walls took her breath away, towering upward in interlocking blocks of carefully dressed limestone. The tangle of forest had been cleared in a broad swath around them, so the sun hammered down on the line of aluxob with their grain and vay sotz with their packs of goods to trade, all waiting to pass through the gates. Neniza joined them, thirsty and footsore; she was unused to walking barefoot and masked on the hard, pounded dirt of the road. A few of the other travelers glanced at her incuriously, but most disregarded her, intent on their destination. She was grateful for their inattention.

Inside the walls she found a clamoring chaos that took the breath right out of her lungs. Smells, sights, sounds, people pushing at her on every side, dogs underfoot, jostling elbows, flapping birds tethered or in cages, sellers shouting, strangers of every caste packed in like ants, and over it all, rearing above the flat level of streets and houses, the imposing heights of the temple and palace mounds.

Neniza stared upward, transfixed, and then stumbled and nearly fell when a passing kisin rammed into her. He continued on without apologizing, while the flow of people buffeted her this way and that, until she lurched up against the mud-brick wall of a potter's shop and stopped to catch her breath.

She could no longer see the palace mound from where she stood, and it was probably just as well. With her goal not dominating her vision, she could calm herself, take slow breaths, reassert her self-control before she ventured back out into the stream of people flowing through the lanes and plazas of the city. They wore shawls and serapes woven in many colors, with beaded fringes of carved wood or even coral, that would have been unimaginable wealth in the villages she knew. It was too much for Neniza to take in. She flinched every time someone brushed up against her, which was often. Never before had she put her mask to such a test, and it was hard to trust that it would hold.

No one gave her a second glance, though. Why should anyone pay attention to a young alux woman, lost in the mass of people swarming through the city streets?

By the time she arrived at the foot of the palace mound, she was breathless and faint, and for the first time she experienced doubt. This was no place for her. She belonged out in the trackless expanses of forest, where the fields and towns had not yet pushed the wilderness back. She belonged in solitude, away from contact with others except when she chose to bring herself near them. She was meant to deal with people singly, not in flocks.

Alone at the base of the mound—for the people of the city did not come here unless they had reason—she bit her lip and looked upward.

The wide steps of dressed limestone led up, and up, and up. The arched entrance to the expanse of the palace mound faced westward, opposite to the main temple, so that the setting sun scorched its carved facade with scarlet light. Two figures stood on either side of the arch; she could not see them clearly at this distance, but their muscled outlines and the spears in their hands marked them as guards. Once past them—if she passed them—she was committed. Or so she told herself. Once she attained the heights of the palace mound, she would not turn back.

Neniza took a deep breath, wiped her sweating brow, and began to climb the steps.

The guards did not move as she climbed past the carved and painted murals of the lord's triumphs against his enemies, but the instant her foot touched the level surface of the smaller landing just below them, their spears snapped across to bar the arch.

Neniza jumped at the movement, even though she had been expecting it. The guards, of course, were ocelotlaca, and she had never been so close to such before. They stood half again as tall as her small alux form, and their muscles slid smoothly beneath the jaguar spots of their fur. They wore loincloths, arm-bands, headdresses of beads and shells; nothing stood between them and harm but their own teeth, claws, and weapons, their skill in battle.

They needed nothing more.

"State your business," a melodiously bored voice said in accented Wide Speech. Within the shade of the archway, just behind the spears, stood an amantecatl. He was dressed in elegant court finery, with golden ear-spools and a pectoral of turquoise and jade. Still, Neniza told herself, he must not be very important, if he were assigned the tedious duty of the palace entrance.

She slid her hands beneath the opposite edges of her shawl, crossing her arms and bowing as she knelt on the hot stone. "I have come to wait in the plaza of the Honored One, in hopes that he will listen to my words."

The amantecatl sighed. "You're going to wait a long time."

Neniza nodded, eyes fixed on a near-invisible seam where two blocks of limestone joined together. "I understand."

"No, you don't," the amantecatl said, and then muttered something in unintelligible Court Speech. "But you may enter, if you wish to waste your time."

A wooden clack as the ocelotlaca tapped their spears together and withdrew them. Neniza rose, bowed again, and hurried through the arch into the plaza behind.

They had grown careless. They believed the threat was long gone. They had not demanded to see her hands.

The amantecatl's words were true. Neniza lost count of how many days she spent waiting in the petitioners' plaza. She knew only how difficult it was to keep her nature disguised, living so closely with others.

She did not need food, but she had to hide her lack of need, and water was a constant concern. Others ran out of provisions but would not leave; they traded sexual favors to the palace-mound inhabitants who came by the plaza, in exchange for what they needed. It was one of the many sacrifices that kept the world functioning. But Neniza, female as she had become, dared not imitate them.

Nor could she maintain the mask forever. Her first task, upon reaching the plaza, was to find an alcove sufficiently sheltered for her to hide in when she felt her flesh failing. The plaza was ringed by buildings, and the petitioners went among them, but privacy was hard to come by.

Still, she endured. She had climbed the palace mound and passed the guards; that meant she could not turn back.

Life in the petitioners' plaza was not a simple matter of waiting. However long Neniza had been there, others had waited longer, arriving after the last visit the lord had made to this place. There were even a few desperate souls who had been there when he came, but had not received the gift of his attention; they stayed on in the fading hope that their fortunes might improve. They were few in number, though. Most who were not heard the first time lacked the determination to go on waiting.

In the plaza, Neniza saw people of every caste. Hairy kisin, owl-eyed chusas, vay sotz with gifts they hoped to give the lord, and at least a dozen aluxob, whose company Neniza avoided. Even some of the noble castes were there, startling her with their presence. Over time she came to understand that not all amanteca and ocelotlaca had courtly rank, that some of their kind had fallen out of favor to the point where they made their way in the cities as commoners, selling their skills to others.

People of every caste except her own.

There were none left in this domain, save Neniza and her father. Still, she found herself searching, looking at the hands of everyone in the plaza, until the day she realized that she was *hoping* to find another, hoping to convince herself that she did not need to be here. It was a desire born of weakness, and so she dug it ruthlessly out of her heart and cast it away. She would not be like her father, and let what had happened pass without consequence.

So she waited, hiding beneath her mask, until her luck finally changed.

"All kneel! All kneel! Kneel before the Master of the House of the Dawn!"

The voice rang out over the petitioners' plaza from the balcony that overlooked it. Neniza glanced up long enough to catch sight of several amanteca, draped in glorious feathered robes and gold jewelry. One, standing forward of the rest, was serving as herald. This much she saw; then, like everyone else, Neniza threw herself to the ground, prostrating herself on the hot stone.

Everything fell silent as the last person grew still. In the hush, they could all hear the measured steps above. The lord of the land had come at last.

The amantecatl spoke again. "Today is not a day for petitions."

What? Neniza thought, and heard someone near her sob once before stifling himself.

"The Revered Lord has come for another purpose," the amantecatl went on. "Three dawns from now begins the feast of the Flayed God, on the day Thirteen Leaf. On this great festival depend our hopes of fertile fields, the growth of the corn which feeds us all. The Elevated One has come here today to seek a maiden to serve as the Rain Bride. The woman so honored will be guaranteed a place in the highest heaven, and the petition she brought with her to this place will be granted. Remain as you are, and he will choose from among you."

Neniza's mind raced as she heard footsteps descending to the plaza. More than one set; of course the lord would not come down here himself. It would be the amanteca, searching among the petitioners for suitable candidates.

She was suitable.

And if they chose her...

She could wait for another day, but there was no guarantee the lord would ever hear her petition, let alone grant it. This would bypass uncertainty entirely—but at a price.

I knew what I risked, coming here, Neniza thought, trembling with excitement and fear. *I always knew.*

She prayed silently as the footsteps ranged up and down the plaza. People said of her kind that they could manipulate others, driving them to think with passion instead of reason. Even Neniza didn't know if it was true. Her father would never answer when she asked—afraid, perhaps, of what she might do with it as a daughter. If it were possible, she had no idea how. But she prayed, as if her thoughts could reach the minds of the amanteca searching the plaza. *Choose me, choose me, choose me...*

One set of feet stopped not far away. Neniza ceased to breathe.

A rustle of feathered robe, as if the amantecatl were gesturing. From above, a soft, sibilant response in Court Speech, and Neniza's skin tingled at the sound of the lord's voice.

"Maiden," the amantecatl said, "the lord favors you."

Neniza risked the tiniest shift of her head. And she saw that the amantecatl was gesturing, not at her, but at a young alux woman less than a pace in front of her.

No. This may be my only chance.

"I beg your forgiveness for my presumption."

The words came out before Neniza could even decide whether to speak or stay silent. All around her, she felt others jerk in horror; they would have edged away, had they not feared to move. As well they might. Neniza would have taken back the words, but she could not; there was nothing to do but speak on.

She lifted her head just enough to speak clearly. To look up would only ensure her death, with the lord standing above. "I beg your mercy. But the woman you have chosen is no maiden."

It was true. Like many others in the plaza, the alux had lain with men in exchange for food and water. How much it truly mattered, Neniza couldn't say—surely they'd chosen wrongly before; was that what caused the drought years?—but having heard it so publicly, the nobles could not ignore her words. Everyone here knew the alux was no virgin, and to choose her knowingly would be to undermine their faith in the festival.

Dead silence had followed on her words. Neniza's muscles ached with tension as she waited. Then a chiming rustle as the amantecatl stepped over the prostrate body of the alux he had been considering.

"Are you a maiden?"

"Yes," Neniza said. *Possibly the only one here.*

The amantecatl said something in Court Speech, not to her. A pause, and then the lord responded again. Was he angry? Amused? Neniza strove to read past the alien, unfamiliar facade of his words, to the mind behind it. She might have just killed herself, and achieved nothing in doing so.

"Very well," the amantecatl said. "You will become the Rain Bride."

She wondered, in the four days that followed, whether the alux whose position she'd taken hated her. The lord's gift to the Rain Bride, the granting of her petition, meant nothing to Neniza now.

She would get what she wanted regardless. The alux might have lost her only chance. But petitioners went home again, once they had spoken or given up, and Neniza knew she herself would not. One always made sacrifices, one way or another.

Her status meant she was treated well, even lavishly. It almost became a problem. They brought her delicacies to eat, and she had to find a way to dispose of them without suspicion—not the peccary meat that villagers might eat in the wet season when food was abundant, but jaguar and eagle, the noblest animals of earth and air. For drink she had delicate wines of honey and fruit; her experience with them was limited, and the first night she drank rather too much. But she maintained her mask, and no one suspected.

Before dawn on the final day, an escort of eight ocelotlaca woke her and took her to be bathed.

Low-ranking amanteca had the job of preparing her. Neniza feigned blushing modesty and managed to wash herself, so that no one would examine her too closely. The higher-ranking artisan who took over once she was clean focused on things other than her hands, painting her breasts and belly and groin, draping her in "clothing" that was nothing more than sweetly chiming jewelry, dressing the soft bush of her hair with hibiscus flowers. The blossoms were an unexpected sign of the wealth and power that surrounded Neniza, for they did not bloom in the dry season, and the rains, of course, had not yet begun.

They prepared her, and Neniza curled her hands into fists to hide them from casual eyes. Let them think her nervous. *I am not afraid.*

The procession was dizzying. Her escort carried her palanquin, while twenty more ocelotlaca formed a solid wall that kept the crowd from her. They descended from the palace mound and crossed to the temple mound, and it seemed the entire city was there to see, for the feast of the Flayed God was second in importance to none.

She climbed the temple mound alone, on her own two feet, with the jaguar-men standing guard below. The carved and painted murals on each temple riser showed the gods in their glory, forming the miracles of the world. At the top, following the priests' instructions, she walked four circuits around the worn stone of the exterior altar, then went into the blessedly cool darkness.

Neniza had never seen the inside of a temple. The space was smaller than she expected, given the imposing facade, but it still dwarfed the village shrines she had seen on a few occasions. The back wall was taken up by a hammered gold image of such intricacy that she could not make out half of it; only the World Tree, dominating the center, was clear to her. Copal incense smoked from censers in the four corners, musky and strong. The smell, more than anything, brought home the reality of what she was doing. Copal was the scent of religion. Copal, and blood.

She lay down on the interior altar and waited.

Outside, the clamor of the crowd gave way to melodious singing. The lord's procession was approaching. Neniza listened, every fiber of her body tight. The clack of spear-hafts: the lord had descended from his palanquin, and the ocelotlaca were standing guard. The chime of jewelry: he was outside the door. A sustained note from the chorus: the lord was performing the rite of blood-letting, piercing his tongue. She could smell the acrid tang as he burnt the strips of bark paper now wetted with his blood.

Then he entered the temple.

A petitioner in the plaza could not look at the lord of the land. The Rain Bride could. Neniza sat up on the altar, and saw what she had come so far to find.

They said he could take the form of a tremendous serpent, but right now he was shaped like a man. A tall man, sleekly muscled, without the heavy shoulders of an ocelotlacatl. His skin glimmered, scales reflecting the faint light inside the temple. She could see nearly all of that skin; he wore a loincloth of jade and gold, and a pectoral, and a drape of pure white cotton hung from his arms, but his body was mostly bare. There was no hair on him anywhere, not even the smooth curve of his skull, but behind him, rustling as he shifted, Neniza could just see the iridescent quetzal feathers that ran down his back.

The sight of him, permitted to her as it was, still sent her to her knees. "Master," she whispered, and slid from the altar to the floor.

The quetzalcoatl who ruled the land came toward her, one sinuous step after another. His presence was overpowering. Not a deity to equal the Flayed God, or any of the others honored in the rituals of the year, but not a person, either. Not like those who waited outside.

Least of all like her.

His voice startled her: not Court Speech, but heavily accented Wide Speech. "Rise, Rain Bride," he said. "Today we are wed."

And so the ritual began.

He would ask for her petition later, when they went outside to complete the ritual, so that it could be publicly heard. But all Neniza wanted was this, here, now: to lie with him, just once. Peasants begged it sometimes, for fertility. The Rain Bride did it for duty.

Her entire body trembled as she rose to her feet, but not with fear. Standing all but naked before the lord, her nature awoke within her. The nature her father fought so hard to keep in check, for fear of what it would do. Male or female, whichever form they took, all of their caste felt it. For males, in the wet season, the passion was different. Safer. Kinder.

Neniza was female, in the dry season, and she was not kind.

She reached out for the feathered serpent, bold with the power that was in her, and drew him toward her, onto her, as she laid herself once more on the altar. Even had this not been their purpose here today, he could not have resisted her. She cried out as he entered her, not in pain, but in triumph.

As he moved above her, she felt her power envelop him. Women of other castes rarely if ever wanted what the males of her kind gave them—the strange, unnerving children they birthed—but it was a gift, freely given. Neniza's rage inverted that power: she gave nothing, and took everything.

Blood dripped from the lord's mouth where he had pierced his tongue. She licked it off her own lips, tasting his life in that blood, feeling it in his body as he rode her. Feeling it flow from him into her. The sensation was intoxicating, exhilarating; she grew drunk with that power, and a laugh built deep within her.

The feathered serpent shuddered above her, spine rippling like water. She put one hand on the scales of his chest to support his weight.

And he froze, staring at the fingers of her hand.

He tore himself free of her more quickly than she could follow, slithering down from the altar to the temple floor. "*Show yourself to me!*"

His voice struck her like thunder. However much she despised him, however much he despised her people, she was a woman of his domain, and he was her lord. She could not refuse his command. The power of it forced the mask of flesh from her at last, revealing what lay beneath.

Skin and muscle gave way to wood. The soft, lush body of a young alux woman dissolved, leaving behind the roughly-hewn form of a xera, like the toys children would sometimes carve for themselves before their mothers saw and took them away to be burned. In shape like a person, but not of flesh, and each hand bore only four fingers, mute testimony to the lesser, inferior, outcaste nature of her kind. She could hide anything with the mask, except that.

He bellowed something in Court Speech, and with a clattering rush the ocelotlaca were there, weapons out. Neniza did not care. She knelt on the floor where his command had left her, and she laughed.

"I am no Rain Bride to be sacrificed," she said, proudly baring her wooden face to them all. "There is no skin to flay from me, no heart to cut out. Your rains can come or not; I do not care."

"I will sacrifice you anyway," the quetzalcoatl spat, his words almost unintelligible through his accent. "I will burn you, as I burned your people."

Her rage could not overcome the power forcing her to kneel,

but she snarled and jerked against it. "My father told me what you did. Yes, we live—you will never be rid of us. Not so long as one male of our kind lives to sire more xera on your women. We are *always* fertile. It is our gift." She laughed again. "But I am not male. Not since I heard the tale of what you did, and knew what it is to want to kill. Where my father gives, I take. And I have taken your life. Within three days you will be dead. Burn me; I am of wood. But I have no blood from which to take your power back."

They bound her there inside the temple, and gagged her so she could mock the lord no more. He sent the priests to choose another maiden from the crowd at the base of the mound; Neniza watched as the quetzalcoatl took her on the altar, then listened as they finished the ritual outside. The girl asked for her family to be cared for. The lord promised to honor her request. Then they cut out her heart and flayed the skin from her to bring the rains, because that was how the world worked; everything that mattered was paid for with sacrifice.

Listening to the drums that followed in the wake of the girl's screams, Neniza wondered if her own blasphemy had tainted the ritual beyond repair. Would there be drought, famine, death?

She did not care. All that mattered was that the lord would not be there to see it.

The signs were already beginning to show when he returned that night. His sleek face was drawn, his delicate scales dulled. The spark that had been in him was in Neniza now, and nothing could take it back.

But they tried. They dragged her from the temple mound back to the palace, and there they ritually abused her wooden body, piercing and splintering it as if she were an enemy noble captured in battle. Neniza laughed at the ironic honor.

She could not bleed, though, and so in the end they did as she knew they must.

The feathered serpent stepped in front of her as they hauled her up. She could see the pyre looming large behind him, and shuddered uncontrollably. Watching her fear, the lord said in grim tones, "You may yet escape it. Restore me, and I will spare both you and your father."

Her father? Neniza would have spat in his face, if her wooden mouth had any moisture in it. She was dry, so dry. Her father was a coward, soft and wet and weak. She would give nothing for his life.

"Take her," the quetzalcoatl snarled at last, his smooth voice distorted with rage and despair.

They dragged her to the pyre and bound her at its peak, and soon the flames danced up around her, licking eagerly at her dry wooden form. She began screaming, then, and did not stop.

But as she died she saw, through the smoke and the wavering air, the lord's withered feathers, ghosting to the ground. And no one, not even Neniza, could tell then if she was screaming or laughing.

But Who Shall Lead the Dance?

IF FATE IS KIND, I shall never see the likes of Elsara Reen again.

Always has it been thus: we faerie folk have our lands, and mortals theirs, and to trespass unbidden from one to the other brings swift retribution. Be it by purpose or chance, if a mortal strays within our grasp, we deal with him according to our ancient ways.

And so it should have been with her.

She was one who came by chance; I know not what odd quirk of fate brought her through our lands. I can only hope it will not do so a second time. But on that summer night, she turned from her path, and we saw her wandering lost in our wood. We guided her steps, by subtle means, 'til she emerged into a glade, and found us waiting there.

I bowed to her and smiled a smile which held no warmth at all. "Have you enjoyed your tour, O mortal child?"

She was not a child; she was a woman grown, a youthful, mortal flower. But to us, she was a mere infant. Weak. Vulnerable.

Doomed.

She knew our ways, but protested still. "I swear to you, I meant no harm. I lost my way—"

"And found yourself here, beneath the summer moon."

"But not on purpose."

"It matters not." My smile grew. "Your name, O mortal child?"

Her eyes flashed fire as she glared at me—my first warning, which I heeded not. "You shall not have it."

"We shall." Forth I reached my hand, and pulled it from her lips. "*Your name.*"

"Elsara Reen," she said; she knew the danger, but could not fight my will.

Wide I spread my arms. "Welcome to the faerie ring, Elsara Reen, mortal child. We care not why you came; you are here. And all who come here face a common fate." The elvenkind had gathered round; I looked at them and smiled. "And what, my friends, might that fate be?"

"She will dance!" one called, his voice the growl of a stalking cat.

"And when will she dance?"

"Tonight!" shouted another, his voice the bay of a hunting hound.

"And where will she dance?"

"*Here!*" shrieked a third, his voice the scream of a hawk on the wing.

And I smiled at Elsara Reen, and asked my final question of her. "But who shall lead the dance?"

She had passion and pride, that would not be cowed by our presence, by our threats. I saw that, and it was my second warning, but I heeded it no more than the first. "You, I suppose."

I laughed, for her spirit pleased me, even as I knew we would break it tonight. "Oh no, mortal child. It is ever the way with us, that guests should have a special place." My own voice cut like winter wind, and I used it as a weapon. "What place more special than this, in the center of our ring? You will dance for us, mortal."

Her eyes went wide with fear, for well she knew what that would mean. "I refuse your judgement. I have committed no crime."

"Dance for us!"

"I shall not!" she screamed.

"*Dance!*"

My command thundered forth, born on a tide of rising sound as our musicians set lip to flute and finger to string. Their music swelled, and the circle about us began to turn, and in that faerie ring at last Elsara Reen began to dance.

Her feet dragged; her arms hung stiff. She fought our call with every strand of herself. But though she fought, still she moved, for never yet was mortal born who could resist our dance.

The music soared higher. Faster. Wilder. I took her hand and led her round, and in the faerie ring we danced, Elsara Reen and I. My feet fell light as dew on grass; hers were the heavy stomps of a clumsy mortal body, weighted by the resistance of a mortal mind. She fought to pull her hand from mine. But once and twice I led her round, and when I spun, she spun with me. When I leapt, she leapt as well. The voices of the flute and harp wove a net in night's chill air, and beneath it all there was the drum, and the fierce swift pulse of the immortal dance.

Her heart sped up. Her breath came fast. Thrice around the circle went, and we two in the center, Elsara Reen and I. Her midnight hair loosed from its knot, one strand, then two, until at last it fluttered free, raven feathers in shadowed night. She fought us still, but we would win. We always did. This price her kind must pay to us; trespassers cannot escape the dance.

The wind rose to a howl, ice-cold and sharp. Naught could save the mortal now; dance she would, until her lungs split, until her heart burst and her blood screamed dying in her veins. I could feel it now. She whirled about the circle with her tresses flying free, and her will too weak to fight. She was ours, a mortal toy, a puppet of the dance.

The howling wind tore clouds away, and shone the moon on the dance below.

Elsara Reen's arms were wide, her face upturned to see the sky. The moonlight silvered her sweat-slick skin, reflected from her wide dark eyes, and I felt then what I had never felt before, in centuries of this game: she surrendered to the dance.

My heart soared then with savage joy, for I did not understand. The faerie music filled the air, the circle spun round faster yet, and in the center there we danced, Elsara Reen and I. We flung our arms out and we kicked our legs high and we spun and we leapt and then, only then, did I see her surrender for what it was: my third warning. Nay, not a warning, for by then it was too late.

Countless times have we done thus, taking in our midst a mortal stray and forcing her to dance until her death. We are immortal creatures, tireless and wild; no human clay can match our faerie dance.

The passion of a human heart, though, burns brighter than any elven soul, and its heat is more than we can bear.

Elsara Reen surrendered to the music, body and soul, heart and mind; she loosed from bonds all the fire of her mortal spirit, and gave it to the fury of the dance.

In the center of the faerie ring, she led us all, and now the lead *was* hers. And we must follow where she led.

Higher she leapt. Faster she spun. Wilder grew her dance.

Bound within the magic of the ring, the musicians played to meet her lead.

The mortal maiden drove them on.

Higher and wilder the music went.

And still the mortal danced.

And with her went our ring. Higher we leapt, and faster we spun, and the wildness of it dragged our bodies after, our spirits caught in burning nets we could not slip free of.

Yet still the mortal danced.

Others felt the terror now. This dance was ours, not the mortal child's. She would dance until she died, driven by our will, and we would weaken not at all: that was how it always went.

But still the mortal danced.

And we began to tire.

Faster and faster round she went. Her feet were as blocks of stone, weighed against faerie flesh; even so, they moved with passionate grace. Her raven hair sliced the wind, deadly and beautiful, signaling doom like a flag. Her mortal heart beat in her breast and it burned with such heat: human life, human fire. It drove us to greater heights, and the players with us, 'til the song was a scream, a sound to give voice to the terror we felt. For we tried to stop, and could not; we tried to break free, and could not. The mortal maiden led the dance.

And she would kill us all.

The air was fire in my lungs, but I drew breath enough to scream, "*Cease!*"

She did.

No few of the dancers collapsed on their sudden release, fainting to the grass among their kin. I held to my feet, but barely, and lifting my head to face Elsara Reen felt like lifting a mountain.

She stood there in the ragged remnants of the circle, and she was not without marks from the dance; her breath came quickly, her skin was flushed, and her arms trembled at her sides. But she stood, when fae had fallen; she lived, when countless mortals before her had died.

She, alone among them, had not fought against our dance.

"And so you made it your own," I whispered, my voice the merest ghost, quiet on the breeze.

"You commanded me to lead," she said, and laughter filled her voice. For all that her ordeal had drained something from her, it had given something in return. What it was, I could not say; the ways of mortals are strange to me.

"We did indeed," I said grimly. "For which folly we have paid."

"And *my* folly?" Elsara Reen smiled at me. She was tired, yes, but there was fire in her still; did we call for it, she would dance again, until none of us could stand against her.

We did not call.

I bowed my head. "Leave our lands. And never come again."

She departed from our ring, and no one tried to bar her way. We did not want her there. Elsara Reen held power over us; she was a danger in our midst. The safest course was to send her on her way.

In the following days, I feared for what her power might mean. Would we now find ourselves at the mercy of every passing traveller? Would our lands be overrun?

But it seems she is unique among her kind, for others have fallen into our hands, and have met with the fate we intended for her. Few mortals have the strength and passion to follow her path.

May it ever be that way.

A Thousand Souls

THE SHIPS ALWAYS hurry away when they see me. Or rather, they try to; I try to make sure they can't. I wish I could call out to them and explain. I'm not some horrible thing, luring men to their deaths simply for the pleasure of it. Killing them is just something I have to do. You see, they have something I need.

No doubt they'd laugh to hear me say that. What could I possibly need? Not food or water; I neither eat nor drink. Not rescue from the rock on which I sit, for the water is as comfortable to me as the air. I have beauty already, with my long golden hair and my perfect pale skin. I have a voice that makes the waves themselves sing harmony. I have immortality; the seas rise and fall, the moon waxes and wanes, the seasons roll endlessly by, but I do not age a day.

They do not have such fortune. They are not so beautiful, and they must eat and drink and age. But I imagine hardly a one of them gives a thought to the precious treasure he carries with him every day: his soul.

I had a soul once. I didn't think of it much, although occasionally a priest would remind me to have a care for its state. They did not approve of my lighthearted ways. But oh, how I wish I had listened to them; those ways brought me to the interest of the sorcerer, and now my soul languishes in a jeweled box, far inland where my lovely finned tail cannot take me.

If only I could have my soul back, I would take such good care of it! I would dress it in the finest silks and sing it sweet melodies. Those men on the ships do not treat their souls nearly so well. They do not know the value of them.

They curse me for taking their souls from them, for drawing their ships in toward the rocks and drowning their bodies in the cold salt waves. I don't know why they complain, though. If it were not me, it would be a storm, or rough surf, or a dozen other things, and then all those beautiful souls would go to waste. They all die, soon enough; do a few days less truly matter?

Just last week, on the dark of the moon, I got thirty-four new souls. It would have been thirty-six, but two swam strongly and made it to shore. I don't begrudge those two. The thirty-four brought my count up to nine hundred eighty-seven, and now another ship is drawing near. It has three masts and a wealth of shining white sails, and I can feel the bright, flickering souls even from here. It's hard to count them exactly, but there's more than thirteen, and that's all I need.

For thirteen will bring me up to a thousand, and a thousand will get me one. The sorcerer for whom I gather these souls has promised it; once I have harvested a thousand for him, from the depths of the sea, then he will return my own soul to me.

I lift my voice in song, and clouds blacken the sky. The waves surge higher, the ship draws closer, and soon it strikes the rocks. In through the cracks floods the cold salt sea, and one by one those bright, flickering souls flutter loose from their bodies. They struggle like little birds as I catch them, for they want to go to the sky, but I cannot let them. They must go to the sorcerer, so that I may be free.

One, two—a few have reached the shore, but it is no matter—six, seven—plenty yet left on the ship—ten, eleven, twelve—

Thirteen.

Fourteen.

Fifteen.

My harvest of souls grows ever larger, and yet my own has not returned to me.

The dying has ended; there are no more souls to capture. I wait, and wait, until the last of the wreckage has washed ashore, and yet the sorcerer does not come.

Could it be I have miscounted? Perhaps it was not nine hundred eighty-seven. It might have been fifty-seven, which would put me now at…nine hundred eighty-three? Eighty-four? Eighty-two? I did not count so closely as I might have. But regardless, I will be free soon.

Unless…

It might not have been *nine* hundred eighty-seven, or even fifty-seven. It might have been *eight* hundred.

Or less?

It's so hard to keep count. The days roll by and I do not age; one ship looks much like another, to my eyes. In the beginning I remembered every one, but now it is so hard.

But that does not matter. I know what I must do. I must keep collecting souls for the sorcerer, until one day I have a thousand, and the thousand will get me one. My very own soul, returned to my keeping.

The sorcerer promised.

Beggar's Blessing

"We beggars come now to your door
Please help us, sir, the humble poor
Charity will fill your halls
Misers have nothing at all."

✧

SNOW HAD FALLEN the previous day and had already turned to grey slush, but flakes drifting down from the sky promised to gild the dreariness with a new layer of white. To Enhardt, it was an unwelcome sight. The first snow of the year was a sign of winter's beginning, and every subsequent one reaffirmed that spring had not yet come. He hated winter, and spent as much of the season as he could indoors, huddled by the fire, counting the days until warmth returned. His scarecrow body felt the cold in its joints, and all winter long he creaked around the house, muttering querulous complaints under his breath. Had he possessed servants, his behavior would have driven them to distraction, but Enhardt had neither maid nor manservant, and so he walked through his cold house alone.

This suited him. He disliked company, especially when he was in a sour mood, and his sour moods lasted all winter.

✧

"Some wine can warm our frozen hands
Guarding them from winter winds

May you have ten times more next year
So we'll get wine again from here."

✧

When the knock came on his door, he scowled. Both the milk and the meat had been delivered already, and he expected no one else save Rinolf Tschauber, who managed his accounts. But Tschauber was not due to come for some time yet, and would never come early. He knew how Enhardt hated unexpected visitors.

For a moment Enhardt considered not answering. But it might be Tschauber, or it might be an important visitor. He rose from his chair, knees cracking, and went into the front hall.

The caller was not Tschauber, nor anyone else important. It was a young woman, her cheeks bright red from the cold, her hazel eyes peering out from under a fringe of untrimmed hair that had escaped her tattered bonnet. The rest of her clothing was in equally poor shape, being little more than layers of patched fabric.

"Bright the night to you, sir, and may Naus Mannein bring you joy," she said, bobbing an awkward curtsy. "Might you have a bit of wine you could spare?"

"Wine?" Enhardt stared at her. Then the rest of her words sank in. Naus Mannein—that damnable evening had come around again. A holiday, they called it. He considered it a bloody nuisance. "No. You can't have any wine."

"Please—haven't you got even a drop to spare?"

"Not for the likes of you." The freezing air was wrapping itself around Enhardt's ankles. He wanted her off his doorstep and gone. Usually they knew better than to come to his house. "I don't give food and drink to worthless layabouts."

She blanched, but kept trying. "I'd sing the Beggar's Blessing for you, sir."

"A bit of annoying song is no kind of payment for valuable stores," Enhardt snapped. "I don't want your blessing."

"But—" She looked confused. Had she never been refused

charity before? "It'll bring you good luck in the coming year."

"I've done quite well without it."

Her wide hazel eyes gazed at him with unexpected seriousness. "Fortunes change. Why take the chance? Do a small kindness, and maybe you'll reap a reward."

"Perhaps your fortunes have fallen, but I'm not so careless as to go the same way." Enhardt had plenty of money set by, plenty and to spare. "I'll go on as I have, thank you. Good evening."

He started to shut the door, but she blocked it with one rag-wrapped foot. "There's a storm coming," she said, her eyes huge and fearful. "More snows, and bitter cold. The storm will come tonight. It will be a hard night, sir."

"Find work, and earn money for shelter," Enhardt suggested. "I understand that most of the prostitutes gather on Tumble Street. I wish you luck in your search for employment." A quick shove on the door made her stagger back, and Enhardt closed it in her face.

Naus Mannein. Enhardt's least favorite time of year. In the days before beggars had learned that his was a household which gave no charity, they'd come to his door by the dozen, asking for food and drink. All the things they were too lazy to earn for themselves. And in return, they'd offer to sing the Beggar's Blessing.

The song was an impertinent piece of work. Enhardt already had it running through his head—no, that was from outside. One of his neighbors must have given that woman wine. Or perhaps it was a different beggar singing; no doubt the swarms had begun to descend. Enhardt scowled and hoped none of his neighbors would be too easily fleeced this year. One bit of charity was bad enough, but the more they gave, the more verses the beggar sang. There was one for wine, and another for bread, and cheese, and ale, and apples…Enhardt stomped back to his desk, mouth twisted into a grimace. Fools, the lot of them. And now he'd have the song in his head for days.

✧

"Some cheese, if you've got aught to spare
It's noble, sir, for you to share
May you have ten times more next year
So we'll get cheese again from here."

⟡

He had scarcely sat down again when the second knock came. Enhardt's eyes narrowed in annoyance. The woman was persistent, was she? Well, he'd teach her not to come to his door again.

But when he opened the door, a different woman stood there. This one was much older, with her hair thickly graying. She gave him a smile that revealed missing teeth. "Bright the night to you, sir, and may Naus Mannein bring you joy. Have you got cheese to spare for a poor old woman?"

"No, I haven't," Enhardt snapped, glaring at her. The woman's smile faltered. "Go away."

The wind gusted strongly at his words, forcing Enhardt to slit his eyes against the ice crystals it carried. When he looked again, the woman seemed to have shrunk in on herself, huddling against the cold. "Just some ale, then, to warm my blood," she begged. "The night will be bitter hard."

Enhardt almost suggested the beggars all get together and sleep in a heap like dogs to stay warm. But he didn't want to start a conversation; he wanted the woman to go away. "Find some other fool to swindle," he said, and shut the door.

Much of the house's warmth had escaped now, and Enhardt's mood darkened as he went back to his chair. He added more wood to the fire before sitting down, but it did little to help. The wind was picking up. It carried the sound of singing to his ears—a child's voice, whether boy or girl he could not tell, soaring high and pure over the moan of the wind.

⟡

> *"A drop of milk can keep us strong*
> *When winter nights are cold and long*
> *May you have ten times more next year*
> *So we'll get milk again from here."*

◆

That voice stayed in Enhardt's mind despite his attempts to get rid of it. He even resorted to humming under his breath, but he could not carry a tune, and outside he could still hear the beggars singing.

But he concentrated on his work, and succeeded in ignoring the noise outside until it was time for Tschauber to come. When the expected knock finally came, Enhardt's mood had improved as much as it could. He rose, added another log to the fire, and went to let the clerk in.

He cursed his carelessness the moment he opened the door. The man on his front step was not Tschauber. He was a gnarled stick of a man, with a face so deeply lined his eyes peered out as if from two caves. They fixed on Enhardt with disturbing directness, but when the man spoke, his voice was so weak it barely reached Enhardt's ears. "Milk, or eggs?" the man rasped. "I haven't eaten in three days."

Enhardt ground the words out through clenched teeth. "I don't give charity. Tell all your friends, and tell them to stay away. The next one of you who disturbs me, I shall chase off with a stick."

The man raised shaking hands in entreaty, but Enhardt closed the door on him. He waited a moment, until he heard the old man shuffle off the steps, then went upstairs to his bedroom to fetch a walking stick. Annoyance heated his blood, keeping him warm in the chill air of his chamber. He *worked* for his living. The cheek of these beggars—expecting free food and drink in exchange for nothing more than a song—roused him as little else could. A meaningless blessing of prosperity, for the stores he'd bought with his own money. What did they take him for?

❖

> *"Good meat puts strength back in our arms*
> *Keeping us alive and warm*
> *May you have ten times more next year*
> *So we'll get meat again from here."*

❖

Pounding came from downstairs. Enhardt had gotten warier; he did not head for the door immediately. Instead he went to the room's tiny window and pressed his face up against the icy glass, peering downward to his front step.

The imperfections in the glass made it hard to see, but the figure outside was much too small to be Tschauber. Enhardt squinted, trying to make out details. It looked like the baker's errand boy. Enhardt had thought the new bread wasn't due until tomorrow, but he might have been wrong.

Nevertheless, he kept his walking stick with him as he went downstairs, and put it in front of him as he opened the door a crack and looked out.

It was a boy on his step, all right, but not the baker's apprentice. The lad gave him a brash smile and said, "Bright the night to you! Got any beef to spare?"

"*Beef?*" Enhardt's mouth fell open at this impudence. "Insolent brat! You think I would spare valuable beef for a street rat like you?"

"Oh, I'm not picky." The boy's grin widened. "Ham would be fine, too. Or hare—I haven't eaten hare in a long time. Even fish, although I'm a bit sick of that."

Enhardt's outrage was such that he didn't even care about the wind blowing into his house, or the snow drifting up against his shoes. "I will not—" he began, but while he was groping for angry enough words, the boy slipped right past him and into the house.

"Hey, nice! Mind if I sit by your fire for a bit? I stopped

feeling my toes around mid-afternoon." The boy dropped himself right into Enhardt's own chair before the hearth.

The walking stick clattered to the floor as Enhardt crossed the room in long strides and grabbed the boy by the ear. "Filthy little guttersnipe," he snarled. "How dare you come in here—sit in my chair—I'll set dogs on you! I'll throw you back down into the sewer you came from!" His face heated with fury.

The boy managed to keep talking even as Enhardt dragged him back to the door. "Just give me a couple of apples, then, and I'll be on my way." His breath hissed through his teeth; Enhardt had yanked harder. "Or jellied cranberries. I'm partial to cranberries. Any fruit, really—" and then they were outside, in the ankle-deep snow.

Enhardt shoved him into the deserted street and roared after him, "Don't even think about coming back! I'll beat you within an inch of your life, you greedy—"

A startled cough brought Enhardt around in the snow. He glared at the muffled figure in front of him before recognizing it as Tschauber, bundled up against the cold. It was only when he saw the clerk that Enhardt realized how bitter the air had grown.

"Is there a problem?" Tschauber asked.

Enhardt did not answer, but stalked back up the steps into his house. A woman approached him from the side, but did not get past "Sir, some vegetables—" before his strides had taken him out of reach. Enhardt waited only long enough for Tschauber to come inside, then slammed the door on the rest of the world.

Tschauber eyed him sideways, but did not say anything. The man knew his job was to keep the accounts, and no more. He sat down in front of the fire and began to spread his papers out, preparatory to making his report.

Even next to the fire, Enhardt felt the cold. And try though he did to focus on Tschauber's words, he could not block out the singing from outside. It sounded like all the beggars in town were out there. He shook his head repeatedly as if that would make the noise stop, and the clerk gave him puzzled looks. Enhardt scowled and told him to get on with his job.

Tschauber went on, but the singing did not stop, and it was starting to drive Enhardt mad.

Finally Enhardt slammed one hand onto the table. Tschauber jerked back, words dying on his lips. Enhardt glared at the walls as if he could see the beggars through them. "I can't think with all that damnable noise," he snarled.

"Sir?" Tschauber said.

"The singing, man. The *singing!* How can you ignore it?" Enhardt stood up; the clerk did likewise, moving more slowly, papers forgotten in his hands. "We will work no more today. Come back next week." He stalked toward the door, leaving Tschauber to gather his things hastily and follow after. "I cannot think," Enhardt repeated, yanking the door open. "Come back when they are gone, when I no longer have to listen to them."

Tschauber stared at him. When Enhardt met his eyes, though, the clerk gave a startled little jump and scurried out into the street, casting one last look over his shoulder before vanishing into the snow-filled twilight.

◆

"We beggars poor ask you for bread
That by your hand we might be fed
May you have ten times more next year
So we'll get bread again from here."

◆

Enhardt shut the door with a bang, but it did not stop the singing. He stood, body tensing, hands drifting toward his head, but they could not block the noise. "*Silence!*" he screamed, shaking with the force of it. "Leave me *be!*"

He pressed his hands to his ears and squeezed his eyes shut, but the song continued, and then an image came to him.

The street outside, coated in white, pristine and unmarred. Not marked by footprints, or even the tracks of a carriage.

Deserted.
There was no one outside.
Enhardt's eyes shot open. Nonsense; it had to be. He heard the singing. But his mind held that image, of Tschauber hurrying down the street, the only living creature in sight.

Slowly, as if of its own will, his hand crept to the doorknob.

He opened the door and the winter wind came in. Enhardt moved out onto the front step, heedless of the cold. He took one stride, and then another, until he was standing in the middle of the empty street. There was no one there, but the singing went on.

The snow blew into his face, freezing his lips, his ears, coating his eyelashes with ice. Enhardt turned a slow half-circle, eyes passing unheeding over the deserted street, until he was facing his house once more.

The singing stopped.

There was someone on his front step. Enhardt drifted closer, feet shoving through piles of snow. Not one person—two. The second lay in front of the door, shrunk into a little huddle, scarecrow arms curled tight around his body, a futile defense against the killing cold.

Kneeling over him was the young woman, the first one. Her hazel eyes were bloodshot and stood out terribly in her white, white face.

"Bread," she whispered through lips cracked and bleeding. "Surely you cannot refuse bread. If not for me, then for him."

Enhardt stared down at the dying man. The skull-like face struck him like a blow. Familiar. The beggar man from earlier. Enhardt couldn't remember what he had asked for.

"This is his last chance," the woman said. Her desperate eyes, full of sorrow and warning, held Enhardt frozen. "Your last chance. This could be you. But you still have a choice."

The singing had stopped. As if the voices were waiting, holding their breath.

The cold had penetrated to the marrow of his bones, leaving no warmth in him.

Enhardt stepped past her, over the man's huddled body, and into his house.

He closed the door, but the house was already as cold as a tomb, and the fire was almost dead. Enhardt passed the hearth without pausing, went to the cellar door, where he lit a candle. This he carried with him down the stairs, to the death-cold room below, where his carefully hoarded food was stored.

Enhardt reached the bottom of the stairs and raised the candle to look around and reassure himself with the sight of the well-stocked room.

It was empty.

He stared, uncomprehending. The bins of fruit and vegetables, the dried meat and fish, the milk and eggs the errand boy had delivered that morning, the wheels of cheese—all gone. He put one hand on a barrel of ale, and it rolled easily at his touch.

Empty.

Only a few crumbs remained on the shelf at his left hand, a mocking reminder of the bread which had been there before he refused the beggars even that.

"This could be you."

Enhardt saw the face of the beggar man from that afternoon as clearly as if he had appeared in the cellar, and it was not the face of the man dying in the snow outside.

His hands rose, shaking, to touch his own face.

The singing had stopped, and would not start again. Inside and out, the air carried frost. Enhardt, alone in his empty cellar, sank to his knees as he felt the first pang of hunger.

Nine Sketches, in Charcoal and Blood

THE TOWNHOUSE of Richard Lowell was not one known to respectable members of Society. He had entertained few guests during his life, and hosted no social events, so all that was known of the house and its contents came through rumour and gossip, whispering of just enough scandal as to be fascinating. Thus, when word went out that Lowell had died, and moreover had died without a will, an unprecedented opportunity arose to investigate the matter—through suitable intermediaries, of course. The public auction was set for May the fourteenth, and many a wealthy man instructed his gentleman-factor to attend, there to observe, and perhaps to purchase any oddities which might appeal.

"Lot forty-one. A clock, bronze, with ivory inlay. Decorated with figures of Egyptian deities. Measures thirty-one hours in the day. Showing here."

A man from the auction firm held up the clock, turning from side to side so that all in the drawing room might see it clearly. The piece was far from the strangest thing yet displayed that day.

"May I start the bidding at twenty? Thank you, sir. Twenty I am bid. Twenty-five, sir. Do I have thirty? Thirty from the lady on my right. *Forty*, sir, very good. Fifty from the lady. Do I have sixty? Sixty-five, sir. The bidding stands at sixty-five. Selling once, selling twice—sold, for sixty-five."

The servant from the auction house bowed to the gentleman in question and moved off to a side room, where his purchase and the price would be recorded. The gentleman and the lady who had bid against him met each other's gazes across the rows of seated figures, and the man nodded gravely to her in familiar salute. He did not look out of place in the room, with his elegant suit and his pale hair neatly smoothed, but to call her a lady was a kindness; she showed every evidence of having fallen on hard times. Her dark linen dress had been made over several years ago with a fair bit of skill, but it was now both worn and out of fashion. Her appearance was not so poor as to forbid her entry to this auction, but she did not look as if she had the wealth to bid on much, and she was so far the only woman to attend. Nevertheless, she sat with her back very straight, her dark head held proudly, as if unaware of or unconcerned with the attention of others.

Neither she nor the other man bid in the next round, nor the one that followed; a statuette of a four-armed Hindu god and a collection of Roman coins in a pane of glass went to two of the gentlemen-factors without much in the way of fuss.

"Lot forty-four. A casket, silver, with vegetative and angelic motifs intertwined. Possibly a reliquary, with relic absent. Showing here. The bidding begins at fifty. Fifty, madam. Do I have sixty?" The auctioneer blinked; it was the only sign of surprise he had exhibited all morning. "One *hundred* from the lady in back. Thank you, madam."

The two who had bid on the clock both turned in their seats, to see who had bid so high.

In the back of the room, a younger woman had entered during the auction of the coins in glass. Her golden hair was fashionably styled and her blue dress was recent; she, at least, appeared to have the means to participate in this affair. She did not acknowledge the presence of either of the two now staring at her, but kept her eyes on the auctioneer, who had continued his monologue with only the briefest of pauses.

"The bidding stands at one hundred. Do I have one hundred ten? One hundred *twenty* from the lady on my right. One hundred fifty from the lady in back. One hundred sixty—now seventy. One hundred eighty. Thank you, madam. Do I have one hundred ninety?"

A tense silence ensued. Even the smartly-dressed gentlemen-factors had unbent enough to wonder at this unexpected escalation.

The shabbier woman was composed, her hand moving from her lap only to signal the auctioneer and, once, to brush an errant strand of dark hair from her face. The lady at the back, though, had grown tense, and her eyes were now locked on the silver casket displayed at the front of the room. Her expression was not that of a woman looking at a costly object.

"The bidding stands at one hundred eighty, from the lady on my right. Do I have—*two* hundred, from the lady in back."

The dark-haired woman's face showed, very briefly, an odd kind of satisfaction. She did not raise her hand again.

"Two hundred I am bid. Selling once, selling twice—*sold*, for two hundred, to the lady at the back."

Murmurs rippled through the audience as the dark-haired woman rose from her chair and proceeded with quick but dignified strides past the victor and out of the room.

The main hall was a bare place, having already been stripped of the paintings that once decorated its walls. Perhaps the auction firm had feared they would disturb the gentlemen-factors, the woman thought ironically. She had not seen them in the listing of items for sale. Which just went to show that the firm had no idea what they were handling. The paintings were harmless. Twisted, but harmless.

"I'm sorry, Elizabeth."

The younger woman had emerged from the drawing room. Elizabeth turned sharply at the sound of her voice, then turned away again, not speaking.

"I couldn't let anyone else have it. I'm sure you felt the same, but my reasons, I believe, outweigh yours." The younger woman gave a dry, unamused laugh. "'Relic absent,' indeed. They're very lucky it is."

Elizabeth spoke at last. "This is more difficult than I thought it would be," she said softly, touching a bare spot on the wall where a picture had once hung.

"I hear you went to the funeral."

"Such as it was. I assume Nathaniel told you?"

"Yes. He intends to be here later."

"Of course he does." A stiff silence followed.

The younger woman was the first to break it. "Do you believe he's really dead?"

"We may as well assume so. Either he's dead, or he will never return to us. I see little difference."

"You can't know that for sure."

"The time for your optimism, Claudia, is over."

Another dry laugh. "Do you think it optimism? I bought the reliquary to ensure no one will ever use it again. I intend to melt it down when I go home. If he should return, I would like not to be taken by surprise."

Elizabeth shook her head. "He won't."

A knock sounded at the front door. Both women turned as a servant from the auction house opened it and took the coat and hat of the tall, thin gentleman who entered. The servant indicated the way to the drawing room, but the newcomer came instead to where the women stood. "Ladies."

"Edward," Elizabeth said. "I imagine we'll have the whole set, by the end."

"All of us who still live," Claudia murmured.

Edward raised his eyebrows. "Are others here?"

"Francis is in the drawing room," Elizabeth said. "And Claudia says Nathaniel is coming."

"Have I missed anything of interest?"

"The reliquary," Claudia said, "and one of the clocks."

"I see." Edward accepted the auction listing from her and perused it. "Nothing significant, then, until the flute. Unless one of you wishes to bid on the astrolabe?"

"Francis may have it, if he wishes," Elizabeth said dismissively. "For all the good it may do him now."

"I was under the impression we were here for nostalgia, not use."

"*I* am here for security," Claudia said, an edge in her voice. "I've just paid handsomely for the privilege of melting the reliquary into bullion."

Elizabeth's lips thinned to a tight line. "We are all here for security."

"But I do believe I shall go back into the drawing room," Claudia said. "I wish to know who is bidding on what—even the unimportant things. Also how much they are bidding. Perhaps I will learn what they're likely to bid, at the end."

"Does it matter?" Edward asked. "'At the end,' as you so obliquely put it, we shall all be bidding every penny we can afford, and likely more besides. It will be enough, or it will not; we shall merely have to see."

Claudia sniffed at his response. "You have become as tedious a fatalist as Elizabeth." With a rustling swirl of blue skirts, she turned and went once more into the drawing room. The steady, genteel drone of the auctioneer's voice drifted out into the echoing emptiness of the hall as the door opened and shut.

Edward watched her go, then faced Elizabeth. "You amaze me. I thought to find you and Claudia at each other's throats."

"My youthful enthusiasm for warfare has waned," she said dryly.

"Is that why you let her have the reliquary?"

"If she cannot banish her nightmares without destroying it, then by all means, let her do so. Else I may have her haunting my door, full of fears of what might happen, as if the time of such matters is not twelve years gone. She even behaves as if Richard might come back."

Edward picked at an imaginary bit of fluff on the sleeve of his coat. "What did happen to him? I've been on the Continent these last years, you see, and only recently returned, so little news reached me—other than that he had passed, and the circumstances were somehow peculiar."

"When did he ever do something in the ordinary way?" Elizabeth glanced at the door the servant had vanished through after admitting Edward, then moved further down the hall. "They found…some few remains, that might or might not have once been part of his body. Those were buried three days ago. Also found were such evidences as held little meaning for those who came upon them, but which—from what I have heard of them—indicate that he was attempting to take up the old ways again."

"Or had never abandoned them," Edward said, supplying the words Elizabeth had left unspoken.

"And now," Elizabeth said, "the vultures gather, to pick over the possessions he has left behind." She shook her head. "I did not expect to mourn their loss so much."

Another knock came at the door; both of them watched as a pair of unfamiliar men were admitted. They hastened into the drawing room, looks of greed and guilty pleasure on their faces at the thought of owning some of the scandalous treasures of so notorious an eccentric.

When the hall was silent again, Edward said, "It is the past you mourn, and not its outward trappings."

As if he had not spoken, Elizabeth said, "They will open the bidding on the flute soon. We should go back in."

She moved down the hall toward the drawing room, her back rigidly straight, maintaining dignity against the stripped nakedness of the walls, the tawdry spectacle of a public auction.

"Elizabeth," Edward said as she reached for the handle of the drawing room door. "Why *are* you here? I don't believe that dress is a costume. You have little money to your name. I imagine we all will risk more than we can afford here today, but for you, the bottom of your purse will be reached much sooner. Are you simply here to see how it ends?"

She turned her dark head just enough to give him the cold, diamond-hard look he remembered from before. Then she went into the drawing room.

Some things, he reflected, did not change after all; and he followed her in.

He saw that Claudia had seated herself at the front of the room, near but not next to Francis Eliot's pale, familiar head. Elizabeth was on the other side of the aisle between the chairs, and well back; Edward chose a seat for himself about level with her, but behind Claudia and Francis. They might all have been friends once—of a sort—perhaps it would be better to say colleagues—but not now.

The flute came and went. Edward bid on it, but half-heartedly; it went to Francis in the end. Senseless, really, to spend money on lesser things, yet they were all doing it. Nostalgia played a larger role here than any of them were willing to admit.

The lots passed, one by one. Francis purchased a gold pendant set with lapis. Claudia purchased an Egyptian scroll. Nathaniel came in, a bony figure in a dark suit, and sat next to Claudia; the two of them leaned their heads together and whispered briefly. Francis purchased a Japanese box. Francis purchased a three-faced figurine. How much money did the man have? Edward found himself bidding on a set of scarabs from a royal tomb, which he did not care about in the slightest, simply to prevent Francis from winning yet another item. He scowled at himself in disgust and went back out into the hall.

He nearly ran down a short, portly fellow who was about to enter the drawing room. "I say!" the man exclaimed, and then each recognized the other. "Edward!" Charles said as the door swung shut. "I'd say, 'What a surprise to see you here,' but it isn't. Have others arrived?"

Edward nodded. "Francis Eliot and Nathaniel Hollis are both inside, and Francis bidding as if he had the royal treasury at his disposal."

"He always was profligate," Charles said, but Edward saw his round eyes narrow slightly, taking in this information. No doubt weighing it against how that might influence Francis at the end. "Just the two of them?"

"Also both of the ladies."

This time the reaction was decidedly visible. "Elizabeth Adams is here?"

"There were but two ladies in our circle," Edward said, watching him. "And neither seems to have transformed herself into someone else. Yes, she's here."

"I shouldn't expect her to show herself at an event like this," Charles said.

"Why not? She seems short on funds, but she *was* one of our number. The only ones I don't expect to see today are Jonathan and Lowell himself, and even then I allow for a chance of that. Who says death can be trusted to keep them away?"

Charles nodded, but his eyes were on the drawing room door, as if he could see Elizabeth through them. "True, very true—but I have heard the oddest things about her."

"Odd?" Edward repeated, and waited.

Charles was still the man he had always been, with a chronic need to talk of what he knew. "Oh, nothing specific. Merely that she is working for...others. Yet no one seems to know who these others may be."

"They must not pay her well, these mysterious 'others' of hers."

"Or perhaps she does not wish to advertise her means. When one looks poorly, no one asks why; it isn't polite. But if one shows wealth, then people *will* inquire, if not directly. They will find out where one's money is coming from. She was always very cautious. I doubt she has changed."

Edward doubted it as well, yet this seemed an elaborate explanation for a simple situation. Which was more likely: that Elizabeth was employed by mysterious figures who paid her well, but hid her wealth, or that she had fallen on hard times?

Or some mixture of the two. "What sort of work do they say she does?"

Charles waved one hand airily. "Skulduggery of some sort or another."

"Elizabeth? *Skulduggery?*" Yet she always had been very practical. And what *was* she doing here today?

Someone knocked on the front door before he could ask Charles more. Edward did not wish to continue this particular conversation in front of a stranger. And even less did he wish to continue it before the familiar figure who proved to be at the door.

"Gregory!" Charles leapt forward, all smiles, and clasped hands with the newcomer even before the servant could take away his hat. "How wonderful to see you. I believe that's all of us, then—except, of course, for Jonathan and Richard, as Edward has so recently pointed out. Ha ha, what a sight *that* would be, eh, if they joined us?"

"Quite a sight indeed," Gregory said, in exactly the level tone he had always used in response to Charles' grating cheer.

Edward gave him a stiff nod. "Gregory."

He received a stiff nod in return, from a head gone white long before its time. Edward remembered the night it had happened, too, and did not appreciate the unintended reminder that Gregory Cabot was not a man to be trifled with.

"Ought to move on in, I should think," Charles said, looking at the auction listing. "Missed quite a few things already, and we're coming up to the end soon enough. Wouldn't want to be standing out here chatting when that comes around, now, would we? 'Twill be quite a show, I should think."

Edward, watching him closely, revised his opinion of a moment before. Charles would never make his fortune at cards, but he had grown better at dissembling; beneath his veneer of empty chatter, he was wary of Gregory. As were they all, and with good reason—even Lowell had been wary of him—but this seemed something more. What else did Charles know, or suspect, that he was not saying? A cold thread of worry crept up Edward's back.

Gregory gave no sign whether he had noticed Charles' wariness or not. "I am not sure we could fail to be present, when the time comes."

Charles laughed, but there was a ragged edge of tension beneath it, not quite completely obscured. "Come, now, do you truly believe it?"

The white-haired man did nothing more than meet his gaze, but the joviality drained from Charles' face. Of course he believed it. Gregory, of them all, would not delude himself into thinking they were not at risk. Elizabeth might be mourning the past, but the past was not entirely dead.

The thread of worry grew colder.

The three of them went into the drawing room, and parted ways inside the door. Edward returned to his former seat; Charles scanned the room, shifting from foot to foot as he spotted the others one by one, before dropping himself into a chair next to the aisle, away from everyone else. Gregory settled himself in just behind Elizabeth's right shoulder, and murmured a brief greeting in her ear.

His entrance had not gone unnoticed. At the front of the room, Nathaniel turned back around in his seat and scowled. "I was hoping he would not show."

Claudia sniffed. "Gregory? Stay away? Not likely."

"He'll have some scheme, though. He always does. I should have killed him years ago." Nathaniel brooded as a small bust of an unknown serpentine god was sold. Claudia seemed serene, but her fingers, wrapped around her reticule in her lap, were tense. There were not many lots left, now.

"You realize," she said to him a moment later, her voice a murmur too low for the nearby Francis to hear, "that if we all truly wished to be secure, we would pool our resources, and ensure that no one in this room would be able to outbid us. Then we could decide amongst ourselves how to dispose of it."

"We don't trust one another enough for that."

"No, we don't. So we bid separately, and if our luck is anything like it was twelve years ago, none of us will win." Claudia glanced at him sideways. "I don't suppose you and I—"

"No," Nathaniel said curtly, and they sat in silence as a shrunken skull came up for bid.

The day was drawing to a close; the light in the room was fading. Servants came in to tend the gas lamps as the auctioneer sold off, one by one, the remaining items from Richard Lowell's estate. The audience thinned out; many of the gentlemen-factors, having bid on and won or lost those items which their masters had sent them to acquire, departed. Others remained, however—some with their purses hardly touched.

"Lot ninety-nine. A leather-bound book, containing nine sketches in charcoal and red pigment, depicting unknown subjects. Showing here."

The man from the auction house held up the book, turning

the pages slowly so the audience might see. In the glow of the gaslight, the images seemed almost to shift. Several of the men watching leaned forward in their seats, attempting to make out the subject matter of each sketch, but it was impossible; the mind, it seemed, would not hold them. But they were compelling, almost mesmerizing; one wished to look more deeply into them, as if some wondrous secret were contained therein. The red pigment was of an odd shade—perhaps a trick of the light—and those closest to the book could discern a faint, unpleasant smell.

Elizabeth murmured over her shoulder to Gregory, in a nearly inaudible voice. "I have done my part, and risked much in doing so. You had best not fail me."

The white-haired man did not respond.

"May I start the bidding at fifty?" the auctioneer said, and blinked for the second time that day at the hands which shot up around the room. Not a single person present had not bid. "One hundred." The hands rose again. "One hundred fifty."

The price rose, and rose, and rose. One by one, individuals began to drop out; the first to go were the men near the back of the room, those furthest from the book. None of them departed.

The tension in the room was as palpable as it was unexpected. The servants hired for the day exchanged glances of astonishment. Far more valuable objects had gone for far lower prices that day. But the book held a strange fascination, and the seven individuals who had known Richard Lowell exuded such an air of tight-lipped determination—even desperation—that others could not help but feel it, too.

"One thousand," the auctioneer said, and murmurs of shock disturbed the taut atmosphere. "The bidding stands at one thousand. Do I have eleven hundred?"

Claudia raised her hand, and the bidding went on.

An oddity began to touch the proceedings. The bidders began to drop out in larger numbers, even before they reached the limits of their purses, and yet it did not seem to them a natural consequence of the unnatural escalation of the auction. The book could not possibly be worth a tenth of what they were bidding, but still they craved it, and that craving warred against a pressure that strengthened the more they persisted. The air grew close and hot; more than one gentleman in the room mopped uselessly at his face with a handkerchief. Soon only a handful were left, and then only one. He struggled to raise his hand in response to the auctioneer but, turning his head as he did so, locked eyes briefly with Gregory Cabot. The man's face paled; his hand dropped swiftly to his lap, and it did not rise again.

Now only the seven individuals were bidding. When it became apparent that no others would interfere, Elizabeth folded her hands in her lap and watched silently. She exchanged a single glance over her shoulder with Gregory, which the others did not see. Their eyes were fixed on the book.

The strange pressure that had laid itself on the room was still manifest. Charles Quincy, sweat-soaked and wild, ceased to bid. Five were left. Francis Eliot dropped out: four. Then Edward. Then Claudia.

The remaining two men might have been carved from stone, so hard were their expressions. Nathaniel Hollis' bony shoulders hunched as if straining against a great weight. Gregory Cabot sat upright, but stiff as steel. Neither moved except to increase their bid. No one else breathed.

"The bidding stands at three thousand six hundred," the auctioneer said. His voice shook slightly as he went on. "Do I have—"

A muscle clenched in Gregory's jaw, casting a sharp-edged shadow. He signed to the auctioneer, and the air of the room hardened to diamond.

"Five thousand," the auctioneer whispered. He licked his lips and summoned his professional composure to repeat it. "Five thousand, from the white-haired gentleman. Do I have five thousand one hundred?"

Claudia stared at Nathaniel as he trembled in his seat, hands clenched into white-knuckled fists. Her eyes flicked desperately from person to person in the room, disregarding the strangers, but picking out Francis, Charles, Edward. Elizabeth sat perfectly upright, her expression mask-like. Only the rigidity of her neck betrayed her inner state. But she was sitting with Gregory, and could not be looked to for help.

Nathaniel shook his head and slumped down, defeated.

And the pressure lifted.

The auctioneer swallowed. "I have five thousand. Selling once, selling twice—*sold*, for five thousand."

Claudia buried her face in her hands.

The auction was completed. Gregory rose to settle his accounts; so, one by one, did the others. The gentleman-factors and the men from the auction house shook themselves free of the strange atmosphere that had prevailed during the final lot. Too much time in a stuffy room, they told themselves. They would be glad to get out into the air, return to their own homes. Odd business, that—but it was already fading from their minds.

Not so with the others. When they had arranged for those items they had purchased to be sent to their homes, they returned to the front hall to find Elizabeth waiting.

"Gregory would like to speak with you all," she said. "Upstairs."

No one objected to them going deeper into the house; no one seemed to notice them going.

The third-floor room was empty, stripped absolutely bare, and no gaslights had ever been installed there. Elizabeth lit candles and placed them in holders that she had brought, then scattered them around the room so they might have light. There were no windows.

The room lay empty, but the smells remained. Faint, but they reached deep into the mind of each person and called up memories that had not faded at all in twelve years.

"You should have worked with me," Claudia hissed at Nathaniel, shaking with fear. "We could have defeated him—"

"Don't be a fool," Francis said. "Didn't you feel what he was doing?"

"And *you*," Claudia spat, gesturing at him contemptuously.

"Spending all your money on insignificant trinkets—you are a cretin, as you always were."

Francis shrugged peacefully. "I like them. They're pretty."

"*Pretty!*" Charles yelped. "How you can think of a thing like that when—"

But his voice cut off abruptly. Gregory had arrived at last, and closed the door behind him.

Each of them stared hungrily at the book he held. Unperturbed, he crossed the floor to stand at the far wall: the position Lowell had always claimed for himself. The significance was not lost on them.

"Now," Gregory said into the breathless silence of the room, "we finish this."

Edward gathered his composure and said, "What do you intend to do?"

"He's got a plan, I'm sure," Charles said. His voice was ragged and unsteady, all pretense of calm gone. "He always does. Bloody schemer—*what are you going to do to us?*"

From where she stood at Gregory's right hand, Elizabeth said, "He's going to set us free."

Her words produced an instant silence. They stared at her, now, attention briefly off the book. "You can't be serious," Claudia said at last.

Elizabeth met her gaze levelly. "Have you ever known me to be frivolous?"

"I don't trust you," Charles said, his voice still wild. "You're up to something, I know it, you—"

Her voice cut across his. "Trust is irrelevant. You will cooperate, or you will suffer. We are all bound to that book. We may have tried to deny it; twelve years is time enough to convince oneself that it is mere fancy. But I am sure the sight of it has undone that delusion. *We are bound to it.* And Richard would never have released us."

"He was bound to it, too," Edward said. "As much as any of us were. He said release was impossible."

Elizabeth raised one eyebrow at him. "And you believed him?"

Gregory spoke again at last. "Richard was bound, yes, but that was a price he was willing to pay, for the power this book could give him over us, should he but learn to use it. You see, we must all be released, or none can be."

Claudia put one slender hand to her throat, eyes wide with sudden hope.

"So," Gregory said. "I have the book. I also have the knowledge necessary to use it against any of you; I trust my demonstration during the auction has made it clear that I have not forgotten the old ways. My intentions, I assure you, are benevolent—"

"How the *hell* are we supposed to believe that?" Nathaniel demanded, his voice shockingly loud against the room's bare walls. "You stand there and admit you haven't given up the old ways—"

"Do *not*," Elizabeth snapped, "inflict on us your hypocrisy. I know what your intentions were, Nathaniel, and what your recent habits have been." Her eyes were cold as ice as she glared at him across the rough circle they had instinctively formed. "I know how we would have fared, had *you* acquired the book."

Claudia edged away from him.

"As I was saying," Gregory continued, "my intentions are benevolent. I wish to release us all from this bondage. But it cannot be done without your cooperation. As it is in your best interests to obtain release, you will provide me with that co-operation." He paused to let them consider his words. "Are we in accord?"

One by one, they murmured agreement, Nathaniel last of all.

"Then let us begin," Gregory said.

They started with the first page. What Gregory asked of them was not complex; compared to some of their past endeavours, it seemed almost trivial. And yet not a one of them was unmoved when the image on the first page shifted and resolved itself into a portrait of the late Richard Lowell, drawn in charcoal and blood.

They moved next to the eighth page, for Gregory wished to begin with those of their number whose mortal bodies had passed on, but who were still trapped in the pages of the book. Soon Jonathan Matthews' face gazed out at them. Then, page by page, through the rest of them. Nathaniel came last, and tried to argue the order, but no one took up his case.

At last all nine of the portraits were transformed, stripped of their protective disorder. The seven surviving members of their old circle each felt naked before the knife, their souls exposed on the pages of the book.

"We have opened the door for each other," Gregory said when they were done. "Now we end this."

And, stepping to his side, Elizabeth lifted the candle-holder no one had seen her pick up, and lit the book on fire.

The pain was instantaneous. Even Gregory's will could not maintain his hold on the book; the burning volume fell to the bare panels of the floor, where it flamed without scorching anything else. Claudia soon followed it, crumpling into a heap of blue skirts and golden hair. One by one, the others collapsed around her. Elizabeth held on the longest, but in the end she too fell, shrieking until she had no breath left. And the voices of the others joined her, both the living and the dead, blending into a single agonizing scream.

Then silence, as the flames died out, the pain ended, and each could breathe once more.

Nathaniel shook his head to clear it, on his hands and knees. Then, faster than thought, he threw himself at Gregory—

But not quickly enough, for Elizabeth was there, with a knife at his throat. "I *will* kill you," she said softly to Nathaniel, and everyone believed it.

Gregory, behind her shielding arm, rose to his feet. "We are concluded," he said. "You are all free to go." He looked down at Nathaniel, who glared at him with crazed eyes. "If you should wish to attempt some working against me in the future, you are free to try, but I would advise you not to. I know what path of study you have followed of late, and it will not avail you. Your soul is your own again; be grateful for it."

Charles was the first to go, stumbling out the door and down the stairs. Francis Eliot picked himself up, straightened his clothing, and offered a bow to both Elizabeth and Gregory before departing. Elizabeth kept her knife out and her eyes on Nathaniel as he backed a few steps away, but she spoke to Claudia. "You may melt the reliquary if you wish. It isn't necessary, though."

"I've been looking forward to it for twelve years," Claudia said. "Why should I pass it up? Don't be an imbecile, Nathaniel; come away." She took him by the arm and all but dragged him from the room.

Now only three remained. Edward looked at Elizabeth, standing at Gregory's side, and thought about what Charles had said, regarding skulduggery.

"You two seem to have been remarkably well-prepared for this," he said.

Elizabeth gave him her driest look. "You need not resort to insinuation, Edward. If you are implying his death was not an accident, you are correct." The knife was still in her hand, and her eyes were cold.

Well, Edward reflected, she always had been a practical woman.

"My thanks to you both, then," he said. "I do appreciate having my soul back. We were fools to ever try that kind of madness." He glanced down at the tiny dusting of ash which was the only remnant of the book and, shaking his head, made his way to the door, where he paused. "If Nathaniel does try anything—"

He stopped mid-sentence, looking at the two of them, Gregory with his unnaturally white hair, Elizabeth with her perfect posture and the knife in her hand.

They could handle Nathaniel.

He tipped an invisible hat to them both. "Farewell."

Then he left the third-floor room for the last time, descended the stairs, and went out into the night.

Letter Found in a Chest Belonging to the Marquis de Montseraille Following the Death of That Worthy Individual

My dearest darling Madallaine,

It is presumptuous of me, you must be thinking, to use such terms of affection in addressing you, for we are at best passing acquaintances, such as would nod and mouth an empty greeting were we to find ourselves at the opera together. I pray you, have patience with me, for the purpose of this letter, which I write knowing that the sickness now resident in my lungs will soon kill me, is to explain to you why it is that we know each other so poorly—and why such a thing should matter to you. In doing so, I hope I will make it clear why I have begun in so familiar a fashion.

Think back, if you will, to a ball you attended in your sixteenth year. I imagine the intervening time, filled with so very many balls, has blurred the memory, but this one was particularly splendid; it was at this ball that the Duc de Corsevois exhibited the tame lions he had recently acquired. The event lingers in my mind for other reasons, though; on that evening, I first had the pleasure of your acquaintance.

Remember that meeting, if you can. It is burned forever into my memory. You wore a gown of the palest rose silk, embroidered down the sleeves with seed pearls; this was the first time you had been permitted anything so fine, you later confided to me, and I told you that you outshone every lady there, and even the moon in the sky. But the evening was not all pretty compliments and dancing; later that night, I drew you aside in a corner and gave to you a small package, which I begged you to deliver to the Duc. I dared not do so myself, but in our conversation you had impressed me not only with your beauty, but also with your quick wit and level head.

Please, do not dismiss this as the ramblings of an elderly man whose senses have been fogged by illness. I know that you have no recollection of such an encounter, no matter how you search your memory for one. This, too, I shall explain, if you will but read on.

You took the package and saw it safely into the Duc's keeping. And because of that deed, he soon left the country, and by doing so escaped the headsman's block. You were not aware until later that your efforts had saved his life, but I made certain he knew, and he was grateful.

We saw much of each other after that. I confess, I had been in love before, and from my experiences I knew that, within a short while, such heady bliss would fade; soon your presence would cease to light up the room, and a single smile from you would no longer cause my heart to falter. Except that you, my darling, were different; your radiance did not fade. I asked your father for your hand, and soon after we were wed.

I had not ever expected to gain a wife, for my life was not one conducive to domestic bliss. But you knew when you wed me that I had for many years been plotting to overthrow the Usurper who had stolen the throne and replace him with the White Prince, our true king. You, alone of all women I have known, not only agreed with me, but wanted to aid my efforts! Ours was a most peculiar marriage, perhaps, full of schemes and intrigue, but it suited us both admirably; together we worked to remove the Usurper from the throne, and in doing so we were happy.

And then came Azray-sur-le-Mont.

I pray you pardon me if tearstains blur my words; this is not easy for me to recount.

The Duc de Corsevois had sent word that he would soon be returning from his exile with a tremendous army to support his Highness. We knew that Azray-sur-le-Mont would be a key battle, for its lord was one of the Usurper's strongest supporters, and you—ever fearless—volunteered to infiltrate the court there and keep us informed as we prepared to strike the first blows for the White Prince. Without your aid, we would have been blind, but with it, we knew we could prevail.

But when the time came for the battle to begin, everything moved too quickly; suddenly our army was outside the castle walls, and you, my darling, were still inside.

I shall not burden you with the details of the battle; they do not matter now.

What matters is that when we overran the castle, the lord of Azray-sur-le-Mont escaped and fled to the docks. I gave chase, with a small company of men, and thus I learned that your duplicity had been discovered; the lord had taken you hostage, and had you with him as he boarded his ship.

My love, forgive me.

We could not let him escape to warn the Usurper of what we had done. Neither could we allow him to have you as his prisoner; the Usurper is a ruthless man, and would have stopped at nothing to make you tell what you knew. We had to stop the ship from sailing, and the only way to do that was to destroy it.

You saw me, from the deck of the ship, and you knew what I would do.

And so it was, my sweet, that in your nineteenth year your life came to an end; you died in the wreckage of that ship, and I gave the order that killed you.

It may be too much to hope that you have read this far. How can I say you died at the age of nineteen when there you stand, alive and well, a woman in her silver years? We met at the Duc's ball, yes, but nothing more; you delivered no package, saw little of me that night but a brief introduction early on. I made my excuses and departed from your company quite rapidly—no doubt leaving the impression that I found you tedious. The White Prince fought at Azray-sur-le-Mont with only a small army, and he fell, defeated, on the battlefield there. We were never in love; we never wed. I have been, at best, a familiar name, a less familiar face.

Please believe me when I say the events I have recounted to you are not simply a product of my fancy, a dream born of some unrequited longing. All that I have said *did* happen. I saw it, lived through it, from the delirious joy of our courtship and marriage to the soul-rending grief of your death.

I have promised you an explanation, and you shall have it.

You recall the late Comte de la Fourré, I assume? Certainly his name should be familiar to you, although I doubt a lady of your station had his acquaintance. His dubious reputation was not unfounded, I admit, although I would not go so far as to call him wicked. Oh, indeed, I knew him well—as did you, in the time of which I have spoken already. It was he who brought this to pass, that I should remember things which never happened.

I blamed myself for your death. As well I should; were it not for me, you would never have become involved with the intrigues that ultimately led to your demise. Had I not given you that package at the Duc's ball, you would have lived a long and fruitful life.

As indeed you have.

De la Fourré approached me not long after your death, when I was sunk deeply into the mire of grief and guilt. At first I did not believe what he told me; it was too fantastical. In my agony, I believed he was mocking me. He was certainly capable of such. But there was no mockery; his offer, for once, was true. He could grant me the opportunity to undo my mistake. I could go back to that night when I started you down the path to your doom, and make a different choice. I could save you, as I had failed to do at Azray-sur-le-Mont.

There is no reason you should believe my words, but I swear to you by all I hold sacred that they are true.

I returned to that night, the night of the Duc's ball, and I removed myself from your company, and forever thereafter I have avoided you at every opportunity. This was for both our sakes; I respected you too much, and knew that if I became an intimate of yours, sooner or later I would be tempted to bring you once more into my world of intrigue. This had slain you once already. I would not risk it doing so again. And because I still loved you, and remembered you as my cherished wife, it was too painful to be near you and know that we must remain apart.

Thus I have lived my life as if I were an exile. The price, however, is one I have gladly paid. Following your death, I was in a terrible state; I doubt I would have been driven so far as to do myself harm, but I fear I would soon have perished through self-neglect and a simple lack of will to live. Instead, you and I have both enjoyed decades more of life. You have married—though not to me—and borne children, and never known the hideous pain of betrayal, of a husband who orders your death. De la Fourré did me a favor I can never repay. Far preferable for us to live apart than

No.

I have committed the words to the page, but I cannot make myself believe them. My strength is ebbing fast; I fear that I cannot take the time to rewrite this letter. The words will stay. And if what I say next causes you to despise me, then my one, feeble defense shall be that I *did* write those words; I tried to believe them, although I failed in the end.

The words are a lie. We have lived decades longer than we would have, it is true, but we have *not* enjoyed them. I have watched you, my love, from the distance of my self-imposed exile, and I know that you are as wretched as I. Your husband does not respect you, let alone love you; you may have wed into a far wealthier home than I was able to give you, but it has provided you with no outlet for your most excellent mind, much less warmth and affection. You have borne children out of duty, not love, and you despise the Usurper as much as I do. For my part, I have lived my life as a lonely bachelor, deprived of love, thwarted in my attempts to bring the White Prince to the throne, and fearful of what would happen should the Usurper learn of those attempts. But I will pass beyond his reach soon, and so I will say here what I have until now feared even to think: I chose wrongly. You, my darling, were dead, and I surely would soon have followed, but we were blessed with three years of love that were more valuable to me than my decades of misery. We loved, and laughed, and by our efforts we brought peace to this land, and a king who ruled with justice instead of caprice. Better to have lived that time, in the fullness of its joy, than to have passed it up for fear of pain. No—I should not have accepted de la Fourré's help. I curse the day he came to me.

You must think me a monster. How can I claim to love you, yet wish you dead? In my defense, I can say only this: that while you were with me, you knew happiness, and that happiness was greater than the sum total of all the life I have replaced it with. I made the choice for you, though, and for that I must beg your forgiveness.

It is too late change anything. My hand shakes so terribly, I can barely hold the pen. I shall not live much longer, not even to look upon your face before I die. I will leave instructions for you to receive this letter when I am gone. Know that I adore you, my treasure, and if there is any mercy in heaven, we will be reunited there, when the stains of my sins have been purged from my soul.

Your devoted love,
Alentin

From the Editorial Page of the *Falchester Weekly Review*

DEAR SIRS—

I was fascinated by Mr. Benjamin Talbot's brief notice, published in the 28 Seminis issue of your magazine, detailing his acquisition of a preserved specimen from a heretofore undocumented draconic species. As we all know, legends of the cockatrice date back many centuries, but I am unaware of any reputable examples collected before now, either dead or alive. This is a thrilling event for the field of dragon naturalism, and I heartily encourage Mr. Talbot to publish his discovery at greater length, including details such as the manner of its acquisition, the island or archipelago in the Broken Sea where such beasts may be found, and a thorough description of its anatomy. An engraving to accompany this article would not go amiss—though naturally a public presentation of his find would be even more desirable. I may dare hope that Mr. Talbot is even now preparing such an article for publication, whether in your magazine or elsewhere, for I have awaited further information with bated breath, and fear I will soon turn blue for lack of oxygen.

I am, as always, your devoted reader,
MRS. ISABELLA CAMHERST

✧

Dear Sirs—

I will beg your leave to respond to Mrs. Camherst through the medium of your pages, for she has addressed me publicly, and as such deserves a public reply, lest I leave your readers in unnecessary suspense.

I assure Mrs. Camherst that my cockatrice will be made public in due course. I am making arrangements even now for its display, which will begin on 21 Caloris in Murtick Square, with admission quite reasonably priced. I hope that she understands my reticence in saying more about its place of origin; the appetite for such curiosities is insatiable, and were I to make public the name of the island where this specimen was collected, hunters might flock to its shores, and the population would soon be reduced to a fraction of its current number. Mrs. Camherst having expressed tender sentiment for the well-being of dragons on previous occasions, I trust that her feminine heart will understand my concerns, and not begrudge me this measure of caution.

Your obedient servant,
Mr. Benjamin Talbot

✧

Dear Sirs—

I thank Mr. Talbot for his solicitous attention to the well-being of both cockatrices and my feminine heart, but I had hoped for rather more specific an answer. To explain my position: as some of your readers may know, I recently returned to Scirland following extensive travels around the world, including a lengthy sojourn in the Broken Sea. I do not claim to have visited every island in that region (a feat I am not certain any human can honestly say he has achieved), but my ship called at multiple ports in both the Melatan and Puian regions, and in all these places I made no secret of my interest in creatures of even faintly draconic nature. I studied everything from sea-serpents to fire lizards to the so-called komodo "dragons" of Singkarbau (which proved not to be dragons at all)—but nowhere in my travels did anyone say anything to me of a creature resembling the legendary cockatrice. Given the distance between here and the Broken Sea, and the unsuitability of any part of the cockatrice for use in ladies' fashion, I cannot imagine that hunters would make terribly large inroads on the population there; but there may be scholars who would wish to study them in their natural habitat, and for such individuals the name of the island would be tremendously useful. Elsewise they must search throughout the Broken Sea for this creature, crossing off their list only those islands I myself visited, where I am certain no cockatrices are to be found.

Regardless, I look forward to Mr. Talbot's public presentation of his specimen, which I will be very interested to inspect at the earliest possible opportunity.

Yours in intellectual curiosity,
MRS. ISABELLA CAMHERST

✧

DEAR SIRS—

It was with some dismay that I opened the 29 Floris issue of your magazine to find another letter from Mrs. Camherst gracing its pages. Although her enthusiasm is remarkable, I begin to feel that she is using your publication as a forum for some kind of campaign against me, which might better have been carried out in private correspondence.

I am of course aware of the expedition to the Broken Sea last year, led by my esteemed colleague from the Philosophers' Colloquium, Mr. Thomas Wilker. I do not think, however, that Mrs. Camherst's role in that expedition qualifies her to offer an authoritative opinion on the full complement of draconic species in the region—a fact she herself admits, though she does not let this hinder her from offering such an opinion, regardless. Indeed, many of the stories we have of her actions during that expedition are anything but scholarly in nature.

In light of this, I can understand Mrs. Camherst's enthusiasm for pursuing the origins of my cockatrice. Were she able to persuade anyone to fund her travels, she might return to the Broken Sea and see the creatures for herself. But I regret to say there is an unfortunate air of grasping ambition about her persistence on this topic, as if she wishes to claim the position of authority regarding this species for herself. Perhaps Mrs. Camherst is unaware of the courtesies practiced among gentlemen and scholars, which dissuade us from "poaching" one another's discoveries; if so, then I hope this reply will make them clear, and bring this matter to a long-overdue close.

Your obedient servant,
MR. BENJAMIN TALBOT, F.P.C.

✧

DEAR SIRS—

I pray you forgive me the tone of this letter, which, although addressed to you, is in reply to Mr. Talbot, and is crafted for that audience.

I note that Mr. Talbot chose to sign his second reply (printed in the 5 Graminis issue of your magazine) with his credentials as a Fellow of the Philosophers' Colloquium. Being a lady, I of course have not been admitted to the ranks of that venerable institution— but I like to think that my publications speak for themselves on the question of my scholarly achievements. (I believe the publications that earned Mr. Talbot his fellowship in the Colloquium were on the topic of geology; though of course this does not completely invalidate his observations in the field of dragon naturalism.) As for Mr. Talbot's comment regarding my actions during the voyage of the *Basilisk*, I choose to interpret that as a reference to the events in Keonga; for surely a gentleman of Mr. Talbot's stature would not slander me by alluding to the scurrilous and unfounded rumours which have circulated regarding my private life and interactions with the men around me.

I must, however, correct Mr. Talbot's misapprehension concerning one of those men. He named Thomas Wilker as the leader of our expedition; you will note my use of the plural pronoun there, which I employ with deliberate precision. The expedition was a joint endeavour between Mr. Wilker and myself, in both its planning and its execution. Any who doubt this matter are invited to submit their doubts to Mr. Wilker himself, who will soon set them straight. (He may even, I dare say, do so politely.)

Furthermore, I should like it to be known that I made several attempts to contact Mr. Talbot by more private means but, having received no reply, found myself with no other option but to address him in the pages of your esteemed publication, in the hopes that I might meet with better luck here. If he wishes to avoid public debate in the future, I suggest he inquire into the reliability of his servants, or perhaps of the Falchester postal service, to discover why it is that my letters have apparently not reached his breakfast table. I am certain there can be no other explanation for why my previous queries went unanswered.

With these matters out of the way, let me speak bluntly.

It seems exceedingly peculiar to me that the cockatrice, which is well-known in Anthiopean legend these past thousand years, should be found on an obscure island in the Broken Sea—quite on the other side of the world. Mr. Talbot has not yet advanced any explanation for how our ancestors of the fifth millennium knew of such a creature, when trade even to the nearer reaches of Eriga or Dajin was uncommon and carried out only with difficulty; nor for why it seems to be unknown in the legends of lands closer to its natural range. Furthermore, while there are branches of the draconic family in which feathers are known—the quetzalcoatl and kukulkan of southern Otholé are of course the most famous, but to them I may add the drakeflies I discovered during my expedition with Mr. Wilker to Bayembe and Mouleen—a cockatrice strikes me as a rather different matter. I know of no true dragon or draconic cousin that exhibits both scales *and* feathers, and I must say that I find so hybrid a creature unlikely in the extreme.

I do not, of course, accuse Mr. Talbot of deception. Rather let us say that I must, with reluctance, consider the possibility that he himself has been deceived; that the man who provided him with his specimen (a man, I will note, who has not yet been identified to the public) was either a charlatan, or himself the gull of one such. The scholarly community has been subjected to hoaxes before, and no doubt will be again.

That Mr. Talbot should consider my interest in this matter to be tantamount to poaching is not only insulting, but indicative of a dismayingly proprietary attitude toward scientific knowledge. Our wisdom grows not by staking out claims and defending them against all comers, but by sharing information freely, so that we may work together for the betterment of all. I would gladly cede all credit for the discovery and study of the cockatrice to Mr. Talbot, if only I trusted him to proceed with integrity.

Yours in regret,
MRS. ISABELLA CAMHERST

✧

DEAR SIRS—

I will keep my reply brief, as Mrs. Camherst's vendetta against me has already occupied too much of your publication and the patience of your readers. I take the gravest exception to her accusations against me, and were this the previous century and she a gentlemen, I would not hesitate to call her out. As it stands, I can see no productive end to this debate; and to further engage her would only be to validate her pretensions to scientific authority. This will be the last that you or your readers will hear from me on the matter.

Mr. Benjamin Talbot, F.P.C.

✧

Dear Sirs—

I was delighted to read last week's leading article ["A Cock-and-Trice Story," 30 Caloris—eds.]. I had followed with interest Mrs. Camherst's debate with Mr. Talbot in previous issues, and so it was gratifying to see the conclusion of that tale featured in your publication. I only regret that the name of the man who sold the specimen to Mr. Talbot is still unknown, as any fellow who can convincingly graft the head of a parrot onto the body of an immature wyvern must be very skilled at taxidermy, and I should like to put such talents to more reputable ends. But I thank Mrs. Camherst for her indefatigable pursuit of the truth, and commend her dedication in disguising herself to attend the opening of Mr. Talbot's exhibit, despite his very public opposition to her presence. While I am certain that a lady scholar of her stature has no need of financial assistance, I am taking up a collection to reimburse her for the costs incurred by admission to the exhibit and her subsequent arrest, as a measure of public gratitude. Any who wish to contribute may write to me at No. 14 Harwater Street in Falchester.

Your servant,
Mr. William Penburgh

Love, Cayce

Dear Mom and Dad,

The good news is, nobody's dead anymore.

Maggie says I shouldn't tell you that up front, because you'll freak out over knowing somebody died. *I* say that if I *don't* tell you up front, you'll freak out when I get to the bit where the temple roof fell in, because you won't know we're all alive now. It's better this way, right?

(Starting with this also lets me say: Dad, despite what it's going to sound like, it wasn't Bjartald's fault. So please don't go charging off to Stoneheart Hall, because Helga will only drop you off the Bridge of Granthun Tol again, and then you'll have to bribe the under-gnomes to let you out, and I know Mom's still ticked about the promises you made last time.)

With that out of the way, let me tell you what your only daughter has been up to since she left home, and why she hasn't been writing letters like she promised.

I admit, I wasn't real optimistic when I walked out of the Rose and Crown. Just because you and Helga and Liraiel and Martin were great friends back in your adventuring days doesn't mean your kids will get along, too. Hell, I honestly thought it was the setup for some bard's tragic ballad, and the only question was which of us would go evil and betray the others. Urgoth or Shariel, was my guess, depending on who's writing the ballad. (Not me, of course. I would never *dream* of going evil. Except, possibly, after three straight weeks of listening to Urgoth and Bjartald snore in harmony.)

And that send-off party in the Rose and Crown almost

convinced me to climb out a window and run off on my own. Yeah, it's great that you guys were big heroes once upon a time, with friends from Okwengu to the northern tundra, but you know, I've listened to the stories my brothers tell. Being the kid of the adventurers who killed Irix Fellshadow isn't all it's cracked up to be. For one thing, you and your old pals have enemies in all those places, too, and for another—does the word "pressure" mean anything to you? And my luck, I get old enough to strike out on my own just when Shariel and Bjartald do, too, and then Martin shows up out of nowhere for the first time in years with a not-entirely-human son in tow, so now it isn't just me, it's a whole pack of us, and gee, wouldn't it be great if you kids all adventured together? Just like in the old days!

If I sound bitter, it's because I was. I can hear Mom now: "You should have *told* us, sweetie!" Yes, I should have. Only the Unblinking Eye knows how different things would have been if I had. But what's done is done; I decided to let you go ahead and relive your glory days through me, and for that alone, everything that's happened since is at least partly my fault.

But don't worry—I don't blame myself for all of it. There's more than enough finger-pointing to go around.

So off we go, out the tavern door, with everybody cheering us on, one more merry band of wet-behind-the-ears kids off to save the world. We felt like *idiots*. The instant we got out of sight, Urgoth clammed up (didn't say a word again for three days), Bjartald started complaining that we'd given him more than his fair share of the baggage just because he's a dwarf, and Shariel, to shut Bjartald up and cover for Urgoth's uncomfortable silence, started lecturing us all on the ancient kingdom that ruled the Heartlands four thousand years ago. Off to a great start, we were.

That night we had our first argument, about where to go. Bjartald was full of advice from Helga, and Shariel had these delusions of going after the ghost of Tel Korass—you know, that undead necromancer you guys never got around to dealing with? Urgoth just sat there and stared at the fire, which meant it was up to me to play umpire between "But Mutter says" and "I'm sure we won't have the slightest difficulty." The only thing we agreed on was that we weren't going within ten miles of that corrupt village priest you all were dropping anvil-sized hints about. The only thing more embarrassing than being sent off with an adventuring party your parents put together for you is accepting Baby's First Quest from them, too.

Thank the gods of all our races for Shadyvale, the town we came to a couple of days later, and the bandits that were attacking its caravans. That was something we could manage. Which we did—and then Bjartald, who may or may not have felt he had anything to prove after some comments I may or may not have made about him being a whiner, volunteered to open up the treasure chest because he figured he could deal with whatever trap was on it (where "deal with" translates to "take it in the face"). But those bandits were vindictive bastards; they'd rigged the chest to a booby-trap on the whole hut, and Shariel ended up with a broken arm and a concussion. So much for protecting the wizard, eh?

Yes, I know what you've always said. Helga wasn't the only parent full of advice. And contrary to family legend, I *do* sometimes listen to what you say. So I hereby admit it: you were right, and we need a thief to deal with traps. That's Maggie, who I mentioned before. The most cleverest of halflings, and beautiful, too, with eyes like autumn honey—so she tells me to write, anyway. (She's leaning over my shoulder right now.) Maggie, aka Margarethadel Mapleweather, was the one who guided us to the bandit camp, and after the hut collapsed we offered her a job with us—even if she did fall over laughing when she saw Bjartald's beard was burnt half off.

(Don't worry; it's grown back. But do me a favor and don't tell Shariel's mother about the concussion.)

But you know, not all of your advice is good! "Goblins," you always said, "goblins are good pickings for young adventurers just starting out." After all, that's how *you* did it, back in your day. Unfortunately for us, the goblins are tired of being picked on by baby adventurers. The survivors of that raid you did on the Snaggletooth tribe? They've started a coalition among the goblins of the

Heartlands, recruiting help from other monsters. Which we didn't find out until we went after a nice easy village about two days west of Shadyvale and ended up in the Dragontrap.

And that's where things started to go wrong.

Uh-oh—the caravan's about to leave. If I don't post this now, you'll never get it; there isn't exactly regular mail service in the Wayyir Desert. Yes, I'm in Wayyir. Yes, I know Dad once got his skin peeled off here, and I remember your warnings never to come within a hundred leagues of the place. No time to explain now. I'll write again later, if I can.

Love,
Cayce

✧

Dear Mom and Dad,

Thank you for the care package—even if its arrival made Abu ibn Jaqsa completely panic, because if you could find us (or probably Liraiel—you totally went to her with my last letter, didn't you, even though I asked you not to), then he thought it meant his shield against scrying had failed in the night. Since we're paying him to keep us hidden through Wayyir, I suppose I'm glad he panicked; better than him being asleep on the job, right? I explained about the amulet you had that crazy gnome implant in my hip, but he isn't convinced. (I'm still not sure I am, either. Every so often I think I feel it *twitching*.)

But the healing potions are very much appreciated, as well as the gold. You forgot, though, to include instructions for how to use the petrified dragons' ears, or even what they're *for*. Are they food? Bjartald keeps insisting they're food. And did Helga really not clip some of his hair before he left, in case of serious death? I can believe it of Martin, but not Helga Hammerhard.

Speaking of Martin—I think I did a very bad job, at that send-off party in the Heartlands, of hiding how uncertain I was about

Urgoth coming with us. I want to say it had less to do with what Urgoth looks like, and more to do with Martin appearing out of nowhere with him just a few months earlier; as dubious as I was about adventuring with Bjartald and Shariel, at least I'd been to their birthday parties as a kid. Then again, I might just be fooling myself. It's hard to trust a stranger, but it doesn't get any easier when he has green skin and tusks. Even if they're *little* tusks.

Well, please convey my apologies to Martin. Urgoth has saved my sorry ass more times than I can count, and it was wrong of me to imagine he might one day turn on us. (But I take back nothing I said about Shariel. Oeu bless her pointy little ears, but if any of us are going to go evil, it'll be her, just out of sheer bloody curiosity.) Maybe if Urgoth's mother had raised him among her people, there'd be a problem, but as it stands he's really more human than orc. And you know, orcs aren't entirely bad—for one thing, they've got better hygiene than dwarves. So if you can reassure Martin (subtly!) that his son's a good adventurer, please do. I know Urgoth worries about it.

Anyway, I've clipped hair from him and Bjartald both, though I'm not sure when I'll be able to send the vials back; Abu ibn Jaqsa insists that teleporting them to you will mean our enemies can find us, though I'm not sure I follow his logic. Then again, what do I know about magic? I'm also enclosing some hair from Maggie—I'd feel pretty rude if you guys resurrected us, but left her dead, just because her parents aren't old adventuring buddies of yours.

So, that letter you put into the care package was pretty fascinating: Shariel's trying to figure out how you got it to telepathically scream certain parts only into my head, and Maggie wants to know where Mom learned to swear like that. Is this any example to set for your impressionable daughter? I appreciate that you guys actually kept your promise not to scry on me once I left home (and, more impressively, seem to have made Liraiel keep it, too), but I'm beginning to think I never should have sent that letter. It's done bad things to your peace of mind. There are things you need to know, though, and since there isn't a lot to do while riding across the Wayyir except sleep—the dust-fiends are mostly nocturnal, so I'm up all night defending the camp—I might as well fill you in.

(YES, Mom, I'm getting enough rest. Is nagging like that something they teach in every seminary? Because it's like you shrank two feet and grew a beard, every time Bjartald opens his mouth.)

So we were going after that goblin village, right? Well, they lured us right in, and we didn't see the magic circle until we were standing in it. A beginner mistake, I know, and one that blew up in our faces rather spectacularly. Some robed creature starts chanting—I have no idea what he was; not a goblin, that's for sure—and next thing we know we're halfway across the world and halfway up a mountain. Dad, you'd be proud of me; I took a look around at the vegetation and figured out we must be in the Dragontrap *before* the first dragon showed up to eat us.

For the record: your stories do *not* do that place justice. Maggie almost fell off the ledge we appeared on, and I think she would have had another birthday before she hit the ground. It's kind of gorgeous, really, with all the granite slabs and snowmelt waterfalls. Pity you can't take the time to appreciate it when you're trying desperately to stay alive.

It was around then that I figured out Shariel and her historical lectures are a calming mechanism that kicks in when she's really nervous. No sane creature of any humanoid race would respond to "Oh shit, we're in the Dragontrap" with a perky declaration that the wizards who constructed the trap-spells achieved it by fusing the imperative art-speech of the ancient Rowhaurangan enchanters with the conjurational whatever of the whoevers. Not unless she's trying to keep herself from screaming. But screaming turned out to be kind of inevitable before she got more than twenty words in, because, well, DRAGON.

As much as I'd like to tell you we bravely whacked off its scaly, horned, fanged, fire-breathing head, the truth is we ran like scared little bunny rabbits. Which doesn't work real well on a surface that's more vertical than horizontal: we promptly fell off the ledge. But hey, there are advantages to thousand-foot-drops; they give you time to think! And also to spellcast. Shariel's calming mechanism must work, or else the screaming settled her down, because she managed first to float our fall, then to make us invisible, and with the winds tearing around in the valleys no dragon was going to be able to track us by scent. Of course, floating as we were, the winds also scattered us to hell and gone, and getting back together when you're all invisible and trying not to be found by dragons is a cute trick.

But we managed it, and then we started running again (this time on flatter ground), and kept running until we were past the boundary of the trap-spells. Funny how fast even a halfling and a dwarf can run with dragons nipping at their heels—okay, Bjartald just tried to knock me off my camel for writing that, and I think Maggie's going to knife me in my sleep. Maybe it will appease them if I also say that it's amazing how far an elf—no, on second thought, I don't want to find out what other spells Shariel has up her sleeves, so I'll just stop while I'm, er, behind.

(Urgoth was great, though. And I'm not just saying that because his sword's as big as I am.)

Insert a lot of gloating here about how good I am, getting us out of the Dragontrap without a map or any of the magic weapons you guys didn't give us because we should, and I quote, "have the fun of winning treasure for yourselves." I'd write the gloating out myself, since my ego could use some balm against the bruises it's taken, but we've lost most of our baggage along the road and Abu ibn Jaqsa's stingy with his paper, so I'm trying to keep this short. Also, it would be embarrassing to write all that, then admit at the end that although I got us out of the mountains, I didn't realize how far south we were.

Yeah. We, er, missed Bhuvak, and crossed over into Lunggar instead.

On the bright side, the slavers apparently never saw a halfling before, and thought Maggie was some kind of mutant breed of beardless dwarf. Which she was quick enough to take advantage of, at least for herself; *she* got the royal treatment, by captivity standards, all the way to Phrasom. (Did you know that's the capital of Lunggar? I didn't. And why didn't I? Because Dad, when giving me geography lessons, pointed at the map and said "That's Lunggar, but trust me, hon, you don't ever want to go there," and moved on to places he considered suitable for his daughter to adventure in. Sorry to break it to you, Dad, but I appear to be on a Grand Tour of everywhere you never wanted me to go, and it would be nice if I knew something about the places I'm being teleported and chased and flown and dragged and shadowstepped to.)

(Just kidding about the shadowstepping. So far, anyway.)

So where was I? Phrasom. I'm not sure what happened with Maggie while we were in the slaver pens; we all got crammed into one big cage, and she went somewhere else. But Bjartald found a Gorevyish priest who spoke enough Heartlander to tell us more than we wanted to know about the slavers' plans for us: they were going to whack off Shariel's fingers and cut out her tongue, then sell her as a pleasure-toy, ship Bjartald off to die in a mine, and send me and Urgoth to their gladiatorial arenas. Apparently there's a big market for female gladiators. They didn't think I'd last long, and I wasn't sure whether to be terrified or offended.

Those plans ended up being useful to us, though. They weren't going to mutilate Shariel until a buyer showed interest (because maybe somebody would want to buy an intact wizard, for the excitement of keeping her from killing him? I don't even know), and the mine overseers only come once a month, so those two were safe for the moment. Urgoth and I, not so much, but when they moved us into a different pen with the other would-be gladiators, I found myself truly grateful, for the first time, that you guys really do have friends *everywhere*. This old guy in the pen (not a gladiator himself, but a trainer) turned out to be Ba Xiue—you know, the Lunggarian mercenary you guys helped escape the geas put on him by his employer? Somehow he recognized Martin in Urgoth's face (don't ask me how), and once all the "hey, how's your father doing, oh I'm sorry to hear his orcish romance didn't work out" formalities were done with, Ba Xiue helped us get a message to Maggie.

Whereupon we proved to the slavers that sticking all the would-be gladiators into one pen is a *really* bad idea, even if you don't give them weapons. Where there's a will, there's a way to kill people.

After Maggie picked the lock on the pen and Urgoth led the Charge of the Pissed-Off Prisoners, we were pretty close to home free—for values of "home" that put us on the wrong side of the continent from the actual holder of that title. Sure, some of the guards got away, and sure, they put the entire standing army of Phrasom into the streets, but Ba Xiue's apparently been itching to lead a rebellion, so we let him get on with that, and got out while we could. Aside from the weird tentacled beastie some conjurer sent after our party, we had a relatively easy time escaping Lunggar.

Once we were in Bhuvak, we started looking for a boat to take us to someplace we'd rather be. Which was pretty much anyplace other than Lunggar or the Dragontrap, at that point. But, well, you know pirates, and I don't mean Cousin Eddie, either. And according to Shariel, the storm that caught us while we were fleeing the pirates wasn't normal, it was some kind of magic thing—I didn't understand her explanation, but it has something to do with a wizard casting a dimensional spell under the wrong conditions during a storm? Judging by what it did to us, it's the same thing you guys ran into when you were on vacation in Asterrhion. Thanks to your stories, I knew enough to keep me and the others from being ripped into bite-sized pieces—though not all of the sailors were so lucky. Of course, the downside to the stories is that I also knew enough to dread what would happen after that. Sometimes ignorance is bliss, or at least better than the alternative.

Dammit, Abu etc won't give me more paper. Sorry for tiny scribble. Will mail this on other side of desert. More later.

Mostly in one piece,
Cayce

⟡

Dear Mom and Dad,

Sorry about that gnomish amulet; you must have had kittens when you realized it wasn't working anymore, and it's been a while since my last letter. No need to worry, though; I'm out of Wayyir and into a civilized land, with both mail service and an abundant supply of paper, and while the royal bodyguards did cut the amulet out of my hip, they brought a priest to heal me afterward. We're not only being well taken care of, we're being *pampered*, and let me tell you, it is so very nice after everything we've been through. Contrary to what you told me during those less-than-adequate geography lessons, Dad, Ahuatepec is not actually a bad place.

It's changed since you chased Fellshadow's mist-assassin here. They tell me there was a palace coup about ten years ago, and the priests don't run the show anymore. The new queen is very nice, and they get so few visitors from outside that we're being treated as if we were royal ambassadors. It's kind of like being on vacation, except for the hummingbird-sized mosquitos.

I seem to be the only person who's not sure what to do with my vacation, either. Urgoth's trying to eat his body weight at least once a day—which is not as much as you might think; we've been on short rations for way too long now, and I don't blame him for making up the difference while he can. Bjartald is alternating between sleeping and sampling the local corn beer with a couple of fellow priests. Shariel, who appears to have misunderstood the concept of "relaxation," is attempting to pack five years' worth of magical education into her head, courtesy of this smoking young sorceress who's figured out that arcana's the quickest route to Shariel's affections—if she can get her to put the books down for ten minutes. Maggie…best not to talk about how Maggie's been keeping herself amused.

Hopefully this convinces you that, despite me being in Ahuatepec, I'm not in dire peril, at least not at the moment. With that out of the way, then, let me get back to the dimensional storm.

I can't remember where you guys ended up after Asterrhion, but it seems that for once we were luckier than you. Call the residents of Dibirvedne barbarians if you like—which they are; raw reindeer meat, ugh—but their shamans know all about dealing with astral creatures. They were a bit surprised when we showed up out of nowhere, but it only took them about three days to figure out how to reverse the storm's effects and convert our bodies back into something physical. (Though Bjartald complains that he still doesn't feel entirely solid.) We therefore got to skip the stage where everyone goes batshit crazy—except maybe Maggie, but really, who can tell?

I won't bother writing up what happened after that, since Jass presumably passed along a summary after we showed up at his thieves' guild in Les Leyasulas. (The ice giant was pretty cool, though. Even if it was kind of a piddling giant, compared to the one you killed outside Irix Fellshadow's glacier-citadel.) Jass did give me the requested earful from you two about the lack of letters—but hey, how was I supposed to know Shariel's messages home were expurgated to the point of uselessness? I thought Liriael was telling you everything. (Don't listen to a word Jass said about what we went on during our visit, though. I ask you, who's the bigger idiot: the supposedly responsible elder brother who left the watch commander in the town square wearing nothing but a few parrot feathers and impersonating a chicken, or his sister who is totally not at fault for some random were-rat thief falling in love with her?)

Anyway, in Les Leyasulas we decided it was time to start acting like grown-up adventurers. You and Helga and Martin and Liriael gave us epic tomes full of advice on how to start our adventuring careers, but we were kind of past our bandit-and-goblin days. And we were tired of being flung all over the map for no reason other than a frantic attempt not to die. (Though I finally understand your favorite proverb, Dad, about how real rangers don't bother with maps. It isn't because we have flawless direction sense; it's because you never end up where you planned to go.) We wanted a mission, and found what sounded like a good one: some kind of warlord troubling the dwarves in the Cwrelyn Isles. It was a chance to save something other than our own hides for once, so off we went.

Remember back in my first letter, when I told you the whole people-dying thing wasn't Bjartald's fault? Please keep that in mind through the next bit.

When we got to the islands, we came across a name I think will be familiar to you. Does Saskarezoen ring a bell? Yeah. Whatever you guys did to banish him after you killed Fellshadow, it didn't stick, and he's found a new follower. Or should I say, a lot of followers. About two thousand when we landed on Cwrele Syg, and more by now. Which, if we were smart, would have meant we ran the other way, even if we had to walk on water to do it. But Bjartald rescued this dwarf-girl right after we got there, and she begged him to rescue her father, who'd been kidnapped by Saskarezoen's chief minion—that warlord Jass told us about—who was trying to use him to force all the dwarves to convert. They didn't like the idea of worshipping a demon (can't imagine why), so we ended up in the middle of a war, and those are hard to walk away from. Especially since you didn't raise me to let my friends go splat the first time they do something dumb—or the second time, or the seventeenth.

But we actually had a plan; I swear we did. Maybe the dwarves liked the idea of pitting three hundred of themselves against two thousand crazed demon-worshippers, but I'd prefer not to go out in a blaze of glory when I'm nineteen—or, more likely, wake up in the temple back home with you two sighing and forking over vast amounts of gold to Father Feordin. It's embarrassing, not to mention painful. Plus my brothers would laugh themselves sick. So we decided to strike a deal with

✧

MOM DAD AMULET RETRIEVED SEND LOCKPICKS OR DIMENSIONAL PORTAL ASAP ALSO HOW DO YOU UNPETRIFY A DWARF

✧

Dear Mom and Dad,

You're lifesavers. Almost as much as if you'd resurrected us; from Bjartald's point of view, being turned to stone is as good as being dead, even if it's cheaper to fix. Also, we got out of the dungeon just in time to snatch Shariel away from the queen of Ahuatepec, so you get credit for the assist on that one. We're still not entirely sure if the plan was to sacrifice Shariel or to turn her into a man and then marry her to the queen—Urgoth thinks they were going to kill her so she could be a vessel for the dead guy the queen wanted to marry, and *then* turn her body male, but Shariel starts gibbering any time we ask, and really, it doesn't matter, because we're fleeing Ahuatepec just as fast as we can go. But Six Flower, the sorceress helping us flee, promises she'll get this letter to you. Apparently she also sent along my earlier attempt, the one that petered out mid-sentence when the drugs they'd slipped into my corn beer kicked in. I don't know if that got to you before or after me yowling for help—which Maggie gets the credit for, although where exactly she kept that wind-whisper charm I don't want to know, since the guards stripped us all before throwing us in the dungeon. Either way, the lockpicks and de-petrification ointment were exactly what we needed, so THANK YOU.

That whole "fleeing" thing means I don't have much time to write—I'm scribbling this while huddled inside a hollow tree, hiding from the seriously giant goddamned eagles they have in this part of the world—so I'll just get to the point. I'm leaving Ahuatepec, and headed to worse places, because of that damned business back in the Cwrelyn Isles. The rest of what happened between there and Wayyir would take too long to tell, so I'm just going to hit the key points:

1) It wasn't Bjartald's fault, it was Helga's, for telling her favorite story so damned often—the one where she killed the wyvern by hammering out a pillar so the ceiling fell in on it.

2) It's doubly Helga's fault for not giving Bjartald enough

architecture lessons for him to know which pillar to hit to kill Saskarezoen, instead of everybody else.

3) You guys, however, get hugs and kisses for telling me to make friends with any wandering monk of Osmaitlik I came across. Having buddies in the order helps a lot when it comes time to resurrect four-fifths of your adventuring party.

4) Get one of your crazy gnome friends to invent a convenient way of hauling around four corpses while trying to contact the Osmaitliks. Also a way to keep them from stinking.

5) I'm trying to invent more key points because I don't want to tell you the last one. Ever since I started writing that first letter I've been looking forward to yelling at you, but now that I finally get my chance I don't want to put the words down on the page. You have to promise me you won't teleport after us, and you won't let Helga do it either, or Liraiel, or Martin, or anybody else, because if you do I won't just be dead, I'll be the kind of dead you don't come back from even if your parents have saved a lock of your hair and enough gold to pay Father Feordin, the kind of dead that doesn't lead to fun stories over beers when you're retired and hanging out with your pals down at the tavern, the kind of dead that even an epic quest to the heavenly dimensions or selling your true name to a forgotten god might not save your daughter from. I mean it. Stay away. We'll fix this on our own.

6) Having said that: YOU DIDN'T KILL IRIX FELL-SHADOW DEAD ENOUGH.

Everybody else got flattened to paste in that temple on Cwrele Syg. *I?* Got my soul stolen. We're heading south from Ahuatepec into Sheshab (which is not *quite* a completely uninhabited wasteland since Fellshadow came back from the dead, bound Saskarezoen into his service, and made it build a city there for his new followers) because the demon told me to come fetch my soul if I could. Which is obviously a trap. I'm not dumb enough to miss that. But what else can I do? Fellshadow knows who we are, and he *definitely* remembers how you guys killed him, and if you show up he won't give you a second crack at finishing him off. He'll obliterate my soul and vanish, and then he'll hunt Shariel and Bjartald and Urgoth down one by one and do the same thing to them, and maybe Maggie too just for the fun of it, and I don't want to see who's quicker on the draw, you or him.

It's all okay, though. Yeah, we're walking straight into the bad guy's lair, and yeah, he knows we're coming, and yeah, I'm pretty sure he's a match even for you guys (at least in your mildly paunchy retired state—don't glare at me, Dad, it's true), which means we don't stand a chance.

But don't worry. We Have a Plan.

Totally not going to die,
Cayce

✧

Dear Mom and Dad,

Greetings from sunny Shadyvale! By now you'll have heard whatever mangled version of the story Shariel gave her mother via the mirror-chat they had, so let me clear up a few things. To begin with: yes, the Plan did in fact involve dressing Urgoth in drag.

No, this wasn't Maggie's idea of a joke. Urgoth swears blind it's some incredibly sacred orcish tradition; you'll have to get independent confirmation of that. It got him past Fellshadow's sentries, though, because they were looking for a big guy trying his best to look human, not an orc woman come to join the Wacky Cult o' Demon-Worshipping Fun. As for the eagle, that was *my* idea, even if Shariel's the one who seduced Six Flower into teaching her the spell for controlling them. But I am not to be blamed for the whole "death from above" part of the Plan, and whatever Bjartald claims, him breaking his fall on the weird sculpture in the courtyard was pure blind luck. We didn't even know until later it was the framework for a spell Fellshadow was perfecting, that let him drain souls to fuel his own power. I hear Liraiel aged a century when Shariel told her that: apparently one of the first things they teach you in Wizarding 101 is never to dispel a major enchantment by smashing it with a free-falling dwarf.

Which is a warning I generally endorse. Having a score of shrieking souls suddenly whizzing around the courtyard, playing slalom with random bolts of arcane lightning, isn't a situation most sane people want to be in. But chaos is a great way to level the playing field, and it took us from "almost certain doom" to "fifty-fifty chance whether you live or die," and we won the coin toss. Urgoth had found the statue Fellshadow bound Saskarezoen to, and I managed to knock it down a staircase (even if I did dislocate my shoulder in the process), which according to Wizarding 102 is the recommended way of freeing a demon. Then it was all up to Maggie and her incredibly fast-talking silver tongue. (You always make getting a demon to drag its master off to hell sound as easy as picking off goblin villages, but—well, okay, given our experience with goblin villages, maybe the two *are* comparable, just not in the way I thought.)

And yes, we got my soul back. Fellshadow had been waiting on feeding it to his spell-machine until I got there: the benefit of a sadistic enemy. Though I must say, he had *atrocious* taste in jewelry. The ring he stuck my soul in is one of the tackiest things I've seen in my life.

So we're back in Shadyvale now, enjoying a well-earned rest while Maggie tells a version of our adventures that bears only a passing resemblance to the truth. Did you know she singlehandedly slew a slate dragon back in our brief mountain interlude? Or that she's now personal friends with the Premier Satrap of Lunggar? I sure didn't.

But the vacation won't last long. For one thing, we need to find a priest who can get my soul out of this travesty of a ring and back into my body. For another, it turns out that you have to be a *lot* closer friends with the monks of Osmaitlik than I am to get four resurrections for free, so we're in debt up to our eyeballs, and sadly, there wasn't much loot to be had in Sheshab. In fact, we've seen a terrible lack of shiny things in general, and those few we've had, we've mostly spent and/or lost. Were you always this poor when you were adventuring? I'm beginning to suspect you retired after Fellshadow because you had pots of money to your name, and wanted to quit before some resurrection fee or dimensional fluctuation or pocket-picking leprechaun made it all vanish again.

(I don't suppose you could spare a bit out of one of those pots of money to pay off the monks? No, I can hear Mom now: "If you're enough of a Mighty Adventurer to go to Lunggar even after your father told you not to, you're mighty enough to pay your own bills." I guess I'd better start calculating the hoard-to-effort ratio of the nearest dragon.)

But mainly we need to start preparing for a little trip. You see, Saskarezoen had a price for prying the ring off Fellshadow's finger before dragging him down to hell. Prior to our attack on the fortress, it seems the demon formed a bit of an attachment to Sexy Lady Urgoth.

He's engaged to be married at the end of the year, and we're all in the wedding party.

So we're off to hell in a little bit, where we'll have to figure out some way to jilt a demon without getting ourselves killed. It's possible Fellshadow's soul will be there, too, and that bastard isn't dead enough for my peace of mind.

Wish me luck. I'll send you Fellshadow's head when we're done—or wedding pictures, depending on how things go.

Still miffed about the ugly ring,
Cayce

Afterword

Although there are many kinds of fantasy, and I happily read and write a wide variety of them, I'll admit that tales set in a world other than ours always feel to me like the heart of the genre. I suspect this owes a great deal to Tolkien—not because he's my favorite author (he isn't), but because the genre as a category of publishing was basically founded on *The Lord of the Rings*, which established the notion of "secondary worlds" as a major literary concept. Tolkien wasn't the first person to think of such a thing, but he's the one who made it popular, and thus enabled the career I have today.

Or maybe it has something to do with my academic background. It may come as no surprise, given the pieces in this collection, that my undergrad and graduate studies were in anthropology and folklore. The inspiration for many of my stories comes from those kinds of sources: mythology, legends, fairy tales, different religions and ways of life, and so forth. The first story I ever had success with, a piece that won an undergraduate fiction award, was directly inspired by the reading I had done for one of my folklore classes. I love to take a little seed, some detail of a culture, and ask myself: what kind of story could this drive? Or sometimes: what if this metaphysical concept were literally true? I'll talk more in the individual story notes about what seed each one developed from, but many of them grew out of exactly that sort of question.

A short story doesn't offer much room for exploring a whole world, compared to a novel. In fact, you *can't* explore the whole world; you have to choose just one corner. But that, in its own way, becomes the great strength of a short story of this type: like a solitaire diamond or a photograph of a single rosebud, it invites the audience to focus on the beauty of that single thing. This makes the short story ideal for concepts that might get buried in a larger work...or concepts that didn't really come with an entire world attached.

Why did I call this collection *Maps to Nowhere*, when the whole point is that the stories take place somewhere else? Because of Diana Wynne Jones' novel *Fire and Hemlock*, which is the book that made me decide to be a writer. In that novel, there are two vases that each say NOWHERE, which can be rotated so that you see different parts of the word on each vase: NOW HERE, WHERE NOW, and so forth. "Nowhere" carries particular meaning in that story, and so I reference it here, in homage to its influence on me.

And that concludes my general remarks. For commentary on the individual stories, read on.

Story Notes

NOTES ON "ONCE A GODDESS"

I owe the existence of this story to the summer I spent working for a service called *Anthropological Literature*, which indexes journal articles in anthropology so that researchers can find things on the topics they need. Sometimes I had to skim an article to figure out what keywords ought to go on it...and sometimes I pretended that's what I was doing, because I just wanted to read the article itself.

The piece that inspired this tale was one of the latter. According to the details I scribbled in a notebook, it came from vol. 32, issue 3 of the *Journal of the Indian Anthropological Society*, and it was written by someone named Allen. It discussed a religious tradition found in Nepal: Kumari Devi, the "living goddess" who manifests in a pre-pubescent girl. The girl is the focus of religious veneration until the goddess is deemed to have passed on to a new host; then she goes home to her family.

That would have been interesting enough on its own, but the focus of the article was not on the worship of Kumari. Instead it looked at what happens to the girls after their term as Kumari is done—how they fit back into their communities, what lives they have as adults, and so forth. Unsurprisingly, many of them have a hard time adapting. After all, they've lived a highly unusual life since they were toddlers, and lack many of the necessary skills and knowledges they would have acquired outside the temple (such as how to cook or run a household). That, even more than the religious tradition, is what made my brain light up. What would it be like to be a goddess for years…and then to be told, now you have to be an ordinary girl?

It took me years to write this story, though. I wasn't sure where I wanted to go with that starting question: what *would* Nefret do, after she left the temple? Was I going to tell the story of how she learned to live without Hathirekhmet, or the story of how she became the avatar of the goddess once more? I suspect I had to mature as a writer before I could even do justice to the concept. When I read the article, I was a twenty-year-old college student with a couple of novels and a bare handful of short stories under her belt. When I finally wrote it, I was twenty-eight and had left grad school; I had written probably a million words more, and could at last thread an interesting path between the two possibilities I had originally seen. This is the result.

"Once a Goddess" was originally published in *Clockwork Phoenix 2*, edited by Mike Allen, in July 2009.

✧

NOTES ON "THE MIRROR-CITY"

I mentioned in the notes for "Once a Goddess" that it took me about eight years to write the story, from idea to actual draft. I can't say for certain whether this one beats that record or not, because I can't pinpoint as readily when the inspiration came to me; it wasn't connected to any specific event or context. I just found myself thinking one day about Venice and its canals, and thought it would be neat to write a story about a place like that, where its reflection in the water was another entire city.

The problem is, a nifty idea gets you nowhere without a plot.

Honestly, I thought this concept would wind up in the trunk of ideas that never went anywhere. In 2014, though, I was invited to contribute a story to an anthology called *Shared Nightmares*. I really wanted to participate, so I opened up the file where I list all my unfinished story ideas and started browsing through it to see whether anything jumped up and said "pick me!"

I had a specific goal in mind, actually. One of the other writers contributing to that anthology had recently said some rather bone-headed things about non-binary gender, so I was motivated to put that kind of thing into my own story. And when I looked at the line in my file saying "The Mirror-City—Venice-type setting, reflection is another city" (which really is all I had), it seemed perfectly suited to exploring outside the gender binary. After all, I could write something about the way those two things intersected, the city and its reflection, through the person of the city's ruler.

And as you can see, I wound up writing that story…but not for *Shared Nightmares*. As the title of the anthology implies, its tone was horror—and I could not see any way to write the story I had in mind without making non-binary gender the source of the horror, which is not at *all* what I wanted to do. So I scrapped that and wrote something else entirely ("The Damnation of St. Teresa of Ávila," which is now in my collection *Ars Historica*), which fit the horror theme very nicely. (That one has the faintest hint of gender stuff in it, too—but it's very faint, consisting only of an angel that shows up in male, female, and gender-neutral guises.)

But I finally had a real story to tell, where before I only had a setting. When Mike Allen, editor of the *Clockwork Phoenix* anthology series, funded a fifth volume on Kickstarter, I knew this would be the kind of thing he was looking for—as indeed it was.

"The Mirror-City" was originally published in *Clockwork Phoenix 5*, edited by Mike Allen, in April 2016.

✧

Notes on "A Mask of Flesh"

When I was a freshman in college I took a seminar on Native American mythology with a visiting professor, Dennis Tedlock. I really wasn't ready for it: I hadn't yet learned how to think like a college student instead of a high school student, and didn't get a tenth as much value out of the course as I might have. But I did keep the books...and years later, when I was in grad school, I went back and picked them up, finally doing the reading I had mostly blown off when it was assigned.

This led me in some very unexpected directions. At the time I was playing in a live-action *Changeling* role-playing game, with a character I had decided spent a lot of time traveling and working in Central America. One problem: White Wolf, the company that published *Changeling*, had never said anything about the faeries of Mesoamerica. (This might be a good thing. Their attempt at North American faeries was...less than stellar.) Because I am That Kind of Nerd, I wound up inventing my own, writing nearly an entire splatbook's worth of material about creatures based on my recent reading.

Some time later, I looked at all the work I had done and thought, "I should do more with that." I couldn't publish it as *Changeling* game material—among other things, that game line was long defunct—but I didn't have to; very little of it had anything to do with the game. If I dropped the RPG mechanics and the connection to the modern day, I had a complex and story-worthy setting: a world without humans, populated by creatures born of Mayan and Aztec folklore. This story was the result.

As for where it ultimately wound up...well, the theme you are seeing in these first three stories is not an accident. Like I said in the Foreword, this collection is organized into several groupings, the first of which is stories that are more anthropological in nature. That is the one of the kinds of things Mike Allen tends to pick for his *Clockwork Phoenix* anthologies, and so all three members of this grouping got their debut there. This is the first one I sold to him, and I still bear him a grudge (not really) for making me go through about seven rounds of revision before he accepted the story—each one more and more fine-grained, until I found myself obsessively deleting and then restoring a single comma, half-convinced that my choice would determine whether I sold the story or not. (He later admitted he'd decided to buy it after the first round.)

"A Mask of Flesh" was originally published in *Clockwork Phoenix*, edited by Mike Allen, in July 2008.

❖

NOTES ON "BUT WHO SHALL LEAD THE DANCE?"

Like many of the pieces in this volume, this story is the result of my folklore education, but it's more indirect than most. There's no specific text I can point to and say, "This is what gave me the idea;" instead, it's more the product of osmotically absorbing a large number of things, most particularly ballads and other folksongs. There's a certain metrical pattern that's common to them:

    da-DA da-DA da-DA da-DA
    da-DA da-DA da-DA

One day the phrase "but who shall lead the dance?" wandered into my head. It fits the rhythm of that second line there; it sounded like there ought to be a line before it, something eight syllables long with four stressed beats. It sounded, in short, like the refrain from some kind of folksong.

I don't compose music or write much in the way of poetry or lyrics, so I wrote a short story instead. This one owes a little something to those stories where a human beats the devil in a fiddling contest, and a little something to fairy folklore, where humans may be punished for trespassing on the territory or activities of their supernatural neighbors. It also came out *far* more rhythmic than most of my prose, in a nod to its origins.

"But Who Shall Lead the Dance?" was originally published in issue #34 of *Talebones*, in February 2007.

❖

Notes on "A Thousand Souls"

There's a fiction award which used to be called the Isaac Asimov Award for Undergraduate Excellence in Science Fiction and Fantasy Writing (now it's the Dell Award for same). It's open to college students and recent graduates; you can submit anything you write while in college. My senior spring, I figured that since this was my last window of eligibility, I might as well write ALL THE THINGS. I managed six short stories in two months (a record for me), of which this is the shortest by far. (It did not win the award, but one of the other six stories did, and one I had written earlier got an Honorable Mention—"Calling Into Silence" and "The Legend of Anahata" respectively, now collected in *The Nine Lands*.) As with the previous story, it doesn't have any terribly specific inspiration; it's just the product of reading about mermaids and sirens and such things over a period of years—as well as my tendency to let my mind wander when I'm counting things, causing me to lose track at higher numbers. It was also one of my first experiments with an unreliable narrator, which didn't work with all readers; one of the magazines I submitted it to sent back a reply praising the narrator's "determination and persistence," completely missing the fact that she's committing murder wholesale for a soul she'll never get back. You win some, you lose some.

"A Thousand Souls" was first published in *Aberrant Dreams*, in February 2007.

✧

Notes on "Beggar's Blessing"

With this story, I can at least point a little more specifically to its inspiration. There's a certain category of folksong that probably has some official name I don't know; I think of them as beggar songs. The category includes "Gower Wassail," "A Pace-Egging Song," and one of my favorite Christmas carols ever, "A Soalin'."

The common thread of the songs is that all of them feature the needy begging for charity and promising blessings in return.

So, of course I wonder: what happens if you fail to show charity?

I initially meant for this story to take place in the Nine Lands, a setting I made up a number of years ago (and have written over half a dozen stories in). After I wrote it, though, I wasn't sure it fit, which is why I'm including it in this collection instead. But if I wind up going back to that setting someday, who knows: maybe I'll retrofit this piece into it after all.

"Beggar's Blessing" was originally published in issue #2 of *Shroud Magazine*, in spring 2008.

✧

NOTES ON "NINE SKETCHES, IN CHARCOAL AND BLOOD"

I wasn't a huge fan of the 2004 film adaptation of *Phantom of the Opera*, largely because the show is designed to be melodramatic when seen from a distance, and putting the cameras up in the actors' faces just takes it too far over the top. But there were some parts I liked: basically everything smaller, the little details you don't see when it's on a stage and you're up in the balcony. The opera dancers putting rosin on their pointe shoes (I used to be a dancer myself), all the backstage stuff…and the auction at the beginning, with Madame Giry and Raoul looking at one another across the room. You can see in their gazes the awareness that they are the only two people there who really understand what happened, the significance of all the things being put up for sale.

A few days after I saw that, I get on a plane to Boston for VeriCon. I'm sitting there in my seat, and two characters wander onto the stage of my mind, mid-conversation. They've come together for an auction, as have the others who begin to join them, and I have no idea what's coming up for bid at the end, but I am *very* curious to find out.

This remains one of the strangest stories I've ever written, not in its actual text, but in the experience of writing it. I still don't know half of what went on with Elizabeth and Gregory and all the rest of them—what was in that reliquary and why is Claudia so fixed on destroying it? "If our luck is anything like it was twelve years ago"—what happened twelve years ago? They never told me. Writing this story felt like taking dictation from someone else. The result is frequently oblique…but I like it that way, and I hope you do, too.

Small trivia: because VeriCon takes place at Harvard and I wrote the bulk of this story on my way there, all the characters are named for undergraduate residential houses or freshman dorms. (Gregory) Cabot is one of the Radcliffe Quad Houses; (Elizabeth) Adams, (Charles) Quincy, and (Francis) Eliot are all River Houses, along with (Edward) Kirkland and (Claudia) Winthrop, though their last names are never mentioned in the story. (Jonathan) Matthews and (Nathaniel) Hollis are named after freshman dorms on Harvard Yard; my husband lived in the former and I lived in the latter. And finally, (Richard) Lowell is named for my own River House, where I spent three very enjoyable years.

"Nine Sketches, in Charcoal and Blood" was originally published in issue #70 of *On Spec*, in November 2007.

✧

Notes on "Letter Found in a Chest Belonging to the Marquis de Montseraille Following the Death of That Worthy Individual"

This still holds the record for Longest Title I've Ever Put on a Story, and I sort of hope I never break it.

Oddly, for such a melodramatic little piece, the inspiration wasn't very melodramatic at all. I won't name the TV show in question because I'm about to give a major spoiler for it, but: at one point I was watching a show wherein the protagonist had to order the assassination of his love interest, because all the alternatives involved many more people dying. (This sounds melodramatic, but in the context it was just grim and heartbreaking.) I found myself thinking that if he could go back and not recruit her for the stuff they were working on, he probably would…but then I stopped and did the math. She contributed substantially to averting a number of other disasters; if he'd never recruited her, how many other things would have gone fatally wrong?

This story is the product of that cogitation, the narrative working-out of that alternate scenario. Alentin *does* change the past, and the consequences are not good. I'm not sure what caused him to take on such a dramatic personality—certainly the character that inspired him is *nothing* of the sort—but that's just what came out of my fingers when I began typing. Possibly he had to be dramatic in order to write this kind of deathbed letter.

"Letter Found" (you didn't think I always typed out the entire title, did you?) was originally published in issue #29 of *Abyss and Apex*, in January 2009.

✧

Notes on "From the Editorial Page of the Falchester Weekly Review"

This piece is connected with the Memoirs of Lady Trent, my series that begins with *A Natural History of Dragons*. For those who are curious, it takes place between the third and fourth books, *Voyage of the Basilisk* and *In the Labyrinth of Drakes*.

It doesn't contain any real spoilers, though—which is always one of the challenges in writing short fiction connected to a novel series. In the case of the Memoirs, I also had another question to answer: what perspective should the story be told from? The novels are all retrospective first person, Isabella telling her life's story from the vantage of old age. I didn't want to do that for a short story, though; I wanted some variety. Should it be a newspaper report of something she'd done? Someone else's account of meeting her? Unconnected with the future Lady Trent entirely, and just taking place in the same world?

These questions collided with another thought in my mind, which was that academic rivalries are great stuff and I really ought to have at least one in my series. Enter this story: a dispute (I hesitate to dignify Mr. Talbot with the name "academic"), carried out through letters to the editor in a widely read publication. It's such a Victorian thing to do, and the moment I figured out my format, the rest was just a matter of letting my fingers go. I wrote the entire thing in a single day while touring with Mary Robinette Kowal for the release of my *Voyage of the Basilisk* and her novel *Of Noble Family*.

"From the Editorial Page of the *Falchester Weekly Review*" was originally published on Tor.com on April 5th, 2016—the same day as the fourth novel, *In the Labyrinth of Drakes*.

◆

Notes on "Love, Cayce"

I don't usually write humor.

Stories that have humorous elements, sure. My characters can snark with the best of 'em. But a story whose entire purpose is to be funny? Not my general mode. Which is why the first draft of this story was about half the length of the final; my subconscious kept fretting that it wasn't funny enough, ergo I needed to finish and get out of there before the audience lost patience with me. But of course rushing things didn't help any—in fact, it hurt. The first draft of this piece was not very good. I had to go back and expand all the things I'd skipped over too fast, let myself really explore all the twists and turns, before the story could work.

So why did I set out to write a humorous story, if that's so unusual for me?

The answer lies in a roleplaying game I participated in years ago. I've played a lot of RPGs, but very little *Dungeons & Dragons*, the granddaddy of them all; this was one of the few exceptions. A friend brought me in to play a major side character for her, and

Amaliáce wound up becoming a player-character instead, as I finished out the campaign with my friends.

…then, a little while later, we decided to play a new campaign, where all of our PCs were the children of each other's characters in the previous game. After a whirlwind opening in which we got kidnapped by an evil goddess and wound up in the Underdark and then killed a young green dragon, my PC finally had a chance to write a letter home and tell her parents where she'd gone and what had happened to her. Which got me thinking about what it would be like to really live in a D&D-type world—to be an adventurer and do all kinds of crazy shit and then retire, only to see your kids grow up and follow in your exceedingly hazardous footsteps. I have to imagine that everything you took as normal when you were the one doing it seems a little more alarming when it's your teenaged daughter out there.

None of the characters or incidents in this story are actually taken from our game, but the spirit of it is. And I may at some point write a sequel, if I can figure out how to make it work; the title for that will be "Advice for a Young Lady on Her Way to Hell."

"Love, Cayce" was originally published in issue #22 of *Intergalactic Medicine Show*, in April 2011.

About the Author

MARIE BRENNAN is a former anthropologist and folklorist who shamelessly pillages her academic fields for inspiration. She most recently misapplied her professors' hard work to *The Night Parade of 100 Demons*, a *Legend of the Five Rings* novel, and *The Mask of Mirrors*, the first book of the Rook and Rose trilogy (jointly written with Alyc Helms as M.A. Carrick). Her Victorian adventure series The Memoirs of Lady Trent was a finalist for the Hugo Award; the first book of that series, *A Natural History of Dragons*, was a finalist for the World Fantasy Award. Her other works include the Doppelganger duology, the urban fantasy Wilders series, the Onyx Court historical fantasies, the Varekai novellas, and nearly sixty short stories, as well as the *New Worlds* series of worldbuilding guides. For more information, visit swantower.com, her Twitter @swan_tower, or her Patreon at www.patreon.com/swan_tower.

About Book View Café

Book View Café Publishing Cooperative (BVC) is an author-owned cooperative of professional writers, publishing in a variety of genres such as fantasy, romance, mystery, and science fiction.

BVC authors include New York Times and USA Today bestsellers; Nebula, Hugo, and Philip K. Dick Award winners; World Fantasy Award and Campbell Award nominees; and winners and nominees of many other publishing awards.

Since its debut in 2008, BVC has gained a reputation for producing high-quality e-books, and is now bringing that same quality to its print editions.

Printed in Great Britain
by Amazon